FAR
FROM
SHORE

Kevin Major

Born in Stephenville, Newfoundland, in 1949, Kevin Major graduated from Memorial University and then taught school in several Newfoundland communities. In 1979 he gave up his teaching career to devote more time to writing.

Kevin Major's books have been translated into several languages and have won many prestigious awards — the Governor General's Award for Children's Literature, the Ruth Schwartz Award, the Canadian Library Association Book-of-the-Year Award for Young People, and the Vicky Metcalf Award — and include *Far From Shore, Hold Fast, Thirty-Six Exposures, Dear Bruce Springsteen, Blood Red Ochre, Eating Between the Lines, Diana: My Autobiography,* and *No Man's Land.* He has adapted *Hold Fast* and *Far From Shore* for the stage. Kevin Major lives in St. John's, Newfoundland, with his wife and two sons.

FAR
FROM
SHORE

KEVIN MAJOR

Stoddart

A GEMINI BOOK

Published in 1995 by
Stoddart Publishing Co. Limited
34 Lesmill Road
Toronto, Canada
M3B 2T6
Tel. (416) 445-3333
Fax (416) 445-5967

First published in 1980 by
Clarke, Irwin & Company Limited

Published in 1991 as an Irwin Young Adult Book by
Stoddart Publishing Co. Limited

Stoddart Books are available for bulk purchase for sales
promotions, premiums, fundraising, and seminars. For
details, contact the **Special Sales Department** at the above address.

Canadian Cataloguing in Publication Data

Major, Kevin, 1949–
Far from shore

ISBN 0-7736-7439-X

I. Title.
PS8576.A56F3 1991   C813'.54   C90-095856-1
PR9199.3.M35F3 1991

Cover Design: Bill Douglas/The Bang
Cover Illustration: Albert Slark
Computer Graphics: Tannice Goddard/S.O. Networking
Printed and bound in Canada

*Stoddart Publishing gratefully acknowledges
the support of the Canada Council,
the Ontario Ministry of Culture, Tourism, and Recreation,
Ontario Arts Council, and Ontario Publishing Centre
in the development of writing and publishing in Canada.*

FAR
FROM
SHORE

PART ONE

1

JENNIFER

If our family had a traditional meal on Christmas Eve, it would probably have to be something like saltfish and potatoes, with fried salt pork smothered all over it. But why not lasagna this Christmas Eve, just for a change? I'm the one who's doing the cooking, and besides, this recipe is a really good one; I've made it before in home economics class. I want to have something special.

I know Mom will say she likes it no matter if she does nor not. And Chris, that will devour anything anyway. Dad is the one I'm supposed to be thinking about. Knowing Dad, he probably won't want to go near it, especially considering the fact there won't be potatoes filling up half the plate. Mom says perhaps we should take out a moose steak or something and let it thaw, but I don't answer her, which means I think he should at least be able to try it.

As it turns out Dad doesn't even show up for supper. We end up eating it by ourselves. It takes Chris five minutes before he has the white tablecloth splattered with tomato sauce. A pig, that's about all he deserves to be called. He eats his own and Dad's share too. I hardly open my mouth and neither do they, except for Chris, who thinks he has to act like it's a belching contest. It's just a stupid meal. I wish I had never started it.

Dad is supposed to be here to help put up the tree, too, once supper is over. He doesn't show up for that either, and Chris has to do it, along with putting on the lights, which of course he just about has a fit trying to get done. I have to watch him like a hawk, because he'll never do it right if I leave him alone. I told Mom we should have had the tree up long before this. Who except for a few old people waits till Christmas Eve anymore to put up a Christmas tree?

CHRIS

My son, I can tell you right now, if you let Jennifer get to you, then it's just as well to call it quits. The past few weeks she's been the crabbiest thing on two legs. You wouldn't satisfy her with the tree lights, not in a million years once she gets in the mood she's in now. We got about ten different kinds and she's got this certain order tattooed to her brain and that's just how they have to go on. Two or three times I have a mind to drop the works of them on her head and tell her to go do it herself.

She did make a pretty good lasagna, I suppose I'll say that much for her. We had candles, fancy tablecloth, the whole bit. The only thing we didn't have was a gypsy playing the violin. And the wine, nothing but the best — must have cost close on three bucks. Who says you can't buy cheap wine these days. Well, she did blow her own money on it. Perhaps she had a right to get a little pissed off.

Jennifer, the dear sister of mine, is sixteen. That's one year older than me. And believe it or not, we do get along fairly good. Most times. I mean, what's the fun of it if we can't rake each other down every now and then for a laugh.

When she finally finishes with the tree, and has rounded up a few presents to toss in under it, out she goes to the kitchen and drags in Mom to get her opinion. What she's looking for is praise. I could give her that, but probably she haven't got two years to wait.

"It's beautiful," the old lady says, just as discouraging as ever.

"Thanks," I tell her.

Jennifer digs me with her elbow. "Mom, will you tell him to cut it out."

"Mom, my dear." I puts my arm around her waist and leads her over to the tree. "Mom, what have you got for eyes? Can't you see it's the lights, the lights that makes a tree? Take notice the different colours, see how each bulb is put on exactly in the right place . . ."

"God, listen to Rembrandt," Jennifer says.

"Thank you. I'm glad to see you're impressed."

"Will you two stop it," the old lady breaks in.

"We'll give it up for New Year's."

"Chris!"

"Okay, okay. It's Christmas Eve. Where's your Christmas spirit?" I wraps an arm around her waist again and takes the other one then and holds it stretched out to the side of us. I have a go at this two-step junk that I haven't got a clue about, but it's what I've seen Dad and her prancing around at sometimes when they've come home from a party.

"Chris!"

But I've got her laughing. "Freak out, mother dear, freak out!"

MOTHER

Some other time I'd go along with his old foolishness, but not tonight. I just haven't got the energy. I swings him around a few times and we lands on the couch. If I could help it I wouldn't laugh, but I got to, a little. He gets me mad, but sometimes he's that foolish you got to laugh at him. Lately he's about the only bit of humour we've had in the house.

It's a wonderful job Jennifer's got done with the Christmas tree. She can turn her hand at most anything, that girl can. Chris shuts off all the lights except for what's on the tree and we sits down then for a spell looking at it. It's the quietest time it's been all day. I gets after Chris to go put on Charlie Pride's Christmas record. It's like asking for the moon, until I makes a move to get up and then he goes. Of course he can't do it without making some comment about the record being so old the grooves must a been chiselled out.

We're not sot down five minutes, though, before we hears the back door open. It's got to be Gord. Lord only knows where he ended up to. He left four o'clock to go down to Decker's to get some cigarettes and he haven't showed up back here since.

I might a known what to expect. When I goes out into the kitchen, there he is, slouched down in one of the chairs, half out of his mind. God, that poisons me. He haven't got the sense God give to a cat. And I knows it's useless to say anything to him, not worth wasting my breath on anymore.

But when Jennifer comes out and sees the state he's in, it's not long before she pitches into him. I've told her about that a dozen times.

"Dad, you're drunk again."

"I am not," he says.

"Dad, you make me so mad! How come you never came home to supper? You weren't even here to put up the tree."

"I'm here now."

"We have it all done now."

"Well, you didn't need me then, did ya?"

"But you know that's what we do every Christmas Eve."

"The hell with Christmas Eve."

"Dad! Try to tell me now you're not drunk."

"I'm *not drunk!*"

"You are so. I can smell it over here and it stinks."

Good God, she'll keep it up and keep it up till she drives me right up the wall. I can't stop to the club for a few beer but she's down my throat.

"I'm not drunk I tells ya."

But she's got to have it proved to her. "Give me some bulbs! Where's the bulbs if youse wants the tree decorated! Show me the tree!"

"Dad, sit down," Chris says. "Sit down. We got it all done."

"No, she wants me to help decorate the tree, so I'll help decorate the goddamn tree."

"Gord, it's all done. Now sit down."

I gets up from where I am and I don't make two steps but there's something in front of me to bang into. There's a friggin chair in the way in this kitchen every time you wants to move your ass. Once I'm in the living room, it's not long before they're chasing in behind me.

"Chris, come over here and find me some bulbs."

He looks through a box. He's about the only one you can talk to sensible around here.

"Com'on, com'on, give us one."

He hands me over something with a damn hook that's so friggin small you can hardly see it.

"Here, let me help ya," he says.

"No. I'm doin it myself. The goddamn tree is goin to get decorated."

I got it now. I heads for the tree. It's got enough bulbs on it now that you can hardly find an empty spot. And they needs me to help decorate it then.

The branches is so hard to get a hold of. They got so much decorations on it, and the lights is enough to blind a goddamn seeing-eye dog.

"Gord, be careful."

What the hell do she think I'm doing if I'm not being careful. It's going there this time, by the god.

Shit, I can feel the feet giving out on me . . . and the branches piling in on top! "Jesus Christ, my face!"

2

CHRIS

I knew what was going to happen, I knew it, the way Jennifer was getting on his back again. I knows it's a dumb thing to be at, getting loaded on Christmas Eve, but there was no need to go and make it worse. It's not all the old man's fault. I suppose he got a right to go on a bit of a tear now and then.

Lucky thing we caught him in time. Me and Mom managed to grab him just as he was about to slide to the floor. He scratched up one side of his face as it was, and hauling him back, off came tinsel and bulbs and God knows what else from the branches. We got him to the chesterfield and he had sense enough to stay there then.

But by this time Jennifer is bawling because of the way he frigged up the tree. That dummy. One minute she acts like she's a ton of bricks and the next minute she's on the bawl. Me and Mom figure it's best if we leave the old man alone and not say anything more. He'll sleep it off after a while.

It's ten o'clock and we're all supposed to be going to church at eleven for the midnight service.

I suppose we could miss it, but it's my turn to serve communion and they're counting on me to show up. I've been bugging Mom and Jennifer to go get ready. I tell them to forget about Dad. When he goes to sleep he'll be out of it anyway. What makes Mom change her mind I wouldn't doubt is seeing the trouble I'm going through to put the tree back the way it was. Dad is asleep before I even goes back into the living room. I knew he would be. And once he's asleep after he's been drinking, nothing short of the house caving in will wake him up. He's just like I am for sleeping.

Jennifer's mood don't change much, even after the tree's all fixed. I couldn't care less. She can stay home if she's that contrary. I can't see much difference in it myself from what it was before, except that one of the presents that was under the tree is all squat up. What odds, it's only a box of chocolates anyway. The cheap kind that haven't got a nut in them, only all that gooey crap. In the end she decides to come. What the frig do she want, a medal?

By the time we get to church the place is jam-packed with people. I'm twenty minutes late because I'm supposed to be there before even the choir shows up. I leave Mom and Jennifer in the back of the church and heads off to the side door and into the vestry. When I gets there they've already started lining up for the procession out on the first hymn. Every one of them's got a candle in their hand and Steve is going around lighting each one. The place is a regular hornet's nest. Rev.

Wheaton looks at me when I comes in through the door.

"We had trouble getting here," I says. I gets rid of my coat in a hurry and goes to the closet to search for a cassock that will fit me. I have to get past about a dozen before I comes across one that's right for me.

"Get me a surplice, will ya," I tell Diane who's hanging around looking like she could use something to keep her occupied. Diane is the other member of the fabulous trio. The three of us serve together, sort of a team like. She's not a bad-looking girl, Diane. And she is pretty fast on the surplices.

"What took you so long?" she asks me. "It looked like you weren't going to show up."

"Diarrhea," I tell her, hauling the surplice over my head and fixing up the shoulders even. "Acid indigestion and my hernia was actin up."

"Very funny."

"Here," Steve says, "take this and keep quiet." He hands me a candle.

"Tompkins, old man, this candle is made wrong." I holds up the bottom end to be lit. "There's no wick."

"Chris, that's enough. We don't have much time," Rev. Wheaton says. I didn't figure he was near enough to hear. I cuts out the fooling around.

The organ noises for the first hymn have started. Diane is in front of us, and me and Steve are the last to leave before the minister. The first hymn is

"O Come All Ye Faithful." All the lights in the church are off, except for some in the sanctuary, so the most you see is the candles. I can't sing but I croaks out something or other. With all the thundering voices up ahead, nobody can hear me anyway.

There's some fellows then who got the face to tell you it looks stupid coming out in a long red cassock like that with a surplice down over it. Some'll even call me a bit weird for going to church at all. I tell them to mind their own business.

To be honest though, after two and a half years I've been thinking about giving it up. I feels maybe I've been at it long enough. I don't know. I used to get a bit of a kick out of being up so close to where everything is going on and being able to look down on the congregation, but I've been over that for long ago. Of course there's more reason to it than that. I should be thinking about the religion part of it and everything I suppose, and Rev. Wheaton is depending on me. I don't know, perhaps I will stick with it for another while longer. Besides, I've got to keep on Wheaton's good side if I expects him to ask me to be a counsellor at church camp this summer.

By the time we get back to the house it's after one o'clock. And it's just like I figured — the old man is snoring it off on the chesterfield. You'd think he'd slack off and give his lungs a break.

"Dad." I shakes him on the shoulder a small bit. "Dad, it's almost one-thirty."

"Wha?" He turns his head, his eyes squinting at me.

"Don't you think you better get up and go to bed. You can't stay here like this all night on the chesterfield."

He stares at me for a while before he says much. "Chris, how about gettin me a drink of water?"

When I gets back with the glass, he rises up a bit and drinks about half the water, then falls back down on the chesterfield.

"Dad, you can't go back to sleep. Mom'll have your head. Com'on, I'll give you a hand." And I takes hold of his arm.

I knew I needed something to liven up my night a bit more. Getting 200 pounds to its feet just about does the trick. He keeps his eyes shut. What's the sense of walking the easy way. Shit, and I should a known the doorway wasn't wide enough for two people. "Hang on." I puts him in reverse and tries it again.

Once we're out in the hall, the rest is small stuff. One straight stretch to the bedroom and I topples him over then on the bed. The old lady takes over from there. I don't stick around, but by the sound of things after I leaves they don't go to bed on very friendly terms.

3

CHRIS

No matter how old you get, Christmas morning is always one to look forward to. When I was younger I'd be up at five-thirty or six o'clock at least. One Christmas it was only three-thirty when I woke up Jennifer to see if she would go down the hall to the living room with me. We was half afraid the old fat guy might still be on the loose so we was practically glued onto each other till we got to the living room and switched on the light. Just then Dad yelled out from the bedroom that it wasn't even daylight and get back to bed because Santa Claus wasn't here yet. The old man never could tell a decent lie. We scravelled off back to our rooms, but I didn't care then anyway. I saw what I wanted to see, even if I couldn't get the hands on it for another two hours — a Big Jim Sports Camper. I was a wicked young kid for the vans and the women.

No getting up at five-thirty anymore, especially after not making it to bed till two, but I don't call it Christmas if you don't get up a bit early and tear open a few presents. Say seven-thirty. Who wants to sleep in on Christmas morning? Jennifer for one. I can just imagine the sour look that comes across her face when I knocks on her bedroom door and opens it up a bit.

"Gonna get up or what?"

It looks to me like she's trying to pretend she's asleep. I ask her again.

"What time is it?" she snarls.

"Seven-thirty." Perhaps I should toss her a chunk of raw meat to quiet her down.

"Go back to bed."

"Com'on, it's Christmas morning."

"You know where you can go."

"Com'on. Wait till you see what I got you."

"I can just imagine. Where's Mom?" she says.

"In her room, I spose."

"When she gets up, I'll get up. Now go on back to bed."

"Jennifer."

"What?"

"You know something?"

"What!"

"You're turning into one pain in the neck."

"Oh shut up and get out of the room."

Contrary. My son, contrary is too good a word for that these days. I daresay if she swallowed a nail, it'd come out a screw. Ever since she broke up with Scott you can't look at her sideways.

I thought for a minute that Chris would at least have sense enough to stay in bed for a while. He should know I didn't get much sleep. But I suppose it's just as well to get up. He won't be satisfied till I do.

If I could get outa bed without waking up Gord I wouldn't mind so much. When I starts to move that disturbs him enough that he twists and snorts a few times in his sleep and swings his arm over my side. I've been turned away from him the whole night because the smell of booze on his breath is enough to kill the devil. When I moves some more his hand tries to hold on tighter and then when I tries to push myself away from him to the edge of the bed, it starts feeling around. That's enough of that. I gets out over the edge and his arm flops down behind me.

I hauls on my old bathrobe and opens up the door to the hall. Chris is just coming out of Jennifer's room. When he sees me he ducks his head back in and tells Jennifer to get up.

"Keep your voice down," I says to him. "Do you want to wake up your father?"

"My God, you're a beautiful chick in the morning."

"Yes, I must be, now keep quiet."

"What electrician does your hair?"

He'll fool around and fool around just the same as if it was twelve o'clock in the day. "Chris, you knows you could a stayed in bed a little while longer."

"It's Christmas morning. We always get up early."

Jennifer opens the door then and comes out. "What are we doing up like this?" she says.

"It's Christmas," Chris answers her.

"All you want, I suppose, is to open your presents, just like some little youngster."

"Com'on, before you wakes up your father!" I got no choice but get mad with him. "Sometimes I wish you would grow up."

But then when I tries to get him to go down the hall he won't budge.

"Now what's the matter?"

"I'm not goin now."

"Why not?"

"Because you two are too crabby. You're makin it into the shits of a Christmas morning."

"Chris, stop bein so foolish."

"You need a psychiatrist," Jennifer says. "For God's sake, you're the one who got us up."

"I'm goin back to bed."

And then, as if that's not enough, out marches his royal highness from the bedroom. They worked at it long enough till they woke him up! All he's got on is the bottom half of a pair of long underwear and that's all slewed to one side. He looks like something the dog dug up. He stumbles on past us and shoves open the bathroom door. He bangs up the toilet seat and out floods the vomit. When I goes in, he's on his knees and the mess is half over the toilet seat and on the floor and soaked into the leg of his underwear.

Blessed saviour, that's something to have to face now at seven-thirty on Christmas morning. I looks at Chris and Jennifer, both of them standing up there, almost getting sick. I sends them back to their rooms because I'm in no mood to put up with their rowing. And that's sure and certain what it'll turn out to be if I leaves them alone — a row.

But before a minute is up Chris is back out again. He don't say anything. He hardly looks at me. He goes to the kitchen and comes back with a roll of paper towels. He unwinds out half the roll and spreads it over the mess and then starts in helping me clean it up.

CHRIS

A real winner of a Christmas, right? Makes you wonder if you wouldn't be better off hiding out in a snake pit somewhere for a couple of weeks. Eventually we get around to opening up the presents. By this time, ten o'clock, Mom is in a better mood. She's trying too hard to be in a better mood as a matter of fact. Dad is still conked out in bed I guess.

No surprises from Mom's present. I don't expect much and that's just about what I gets. A new watch — it's digital and it's made to look like it could be expensive, but I can tell it's not. I knows there's not much money on the go, so how

21

can I mouth off. But I don't get very excited either. I try a bit harder on the next gift. It's from Jennifer, but it's the first I've seen of it because she always brings out her presents Christmas morning so nobody will be banging them around, trying to guess what's in them.

I can tell right away that it's a record album. I didn't expect that, to be honest. The way we was getting along last night I figure it should be a tarantula or something. It's done up so fancy I hardly feels like ripping off the paper. The tag's got a chocolate Christmas tree on it.

When I opens it up I gets an even bigger surprise. There's not one, but two albums. I mean they're good ones — Bob Seger and Streetheart. Shit, it's a surprise. I mean I really didn't think she'd spend all that money on me.

"Thanks. Thanks a lot." It comes out a bit weak but I mean it.

She don't say anything. But at the same time I'm sitting there with my mouth open, looking like I got clobbered over the head or something, she takes hold of one of the presents I got for her — the joke one.

"Don't expect much," I tell her. "That one's kind of a joke." After two albums I figure the least I can do is put out some kind of warning.

"Not another one. How many times have you got it wrapped up this year?" Last year I bought her a box of cherry chocolates and three boxes of Ex-lax and wrapped them up about twenty different times till what I had was a present about four foot square. It was a pretty decent laugh. I always give her something for a laugh and then a real present besides.

I've got the box stuffed with newspapers. She expected that and picks up each piece with two fingers like they're contaminated and then tosses them out on the floor. This goes on and on and she starts thinking there's nothing at all in there. It's right down at the bottom.

When she looks at it she don't exactly keel over laughing. I wasn't expecting a roar, maybe just a fake grin. But not even that. What she does is storm off into her room. No shit. So maybe it wasn't such a fantastic idea. It's only one of those fake trophies. With a card saying "World's Greatest Lover" stuck to it.

And then, as if that's not enough, Mom pitches into me once she has a look in the box.

"Chris!"

"It's only a little joke. I got her something else."

"You should be ashamed of yourself."

"I only done it for a laugh. She still can't be that hung up on him."

"I don't see anybody laughing, do you?"

"Okay, so I'm sorry, so just forget about it."

"Forget about it. That's easy enough to say. You tell your sister that."

"I said I was sorry!"

Good God, it's only a stupid present. The old lady is worse than Jennifer when it comes to being contrary. I'm not about to sit there and listen to her yell at me over something like that. I takes off into my bedroom. Frig, it's pretty damn bad when your own family can't even take a joke.

JENNIFER

After a few minutes in the room I'm madder at myself than I am at Chris, the stupid idiot. I should have told him off, that's what I should have done. He knows damn well I still like Scott. He hasn't got any feelings for anything or anybody, that's the problem.

That Chris gets away with too much, if you ask me, because for sure Dad won't say anything to him when he finds out. At the rate we're going this family will soon need its head examined. By next fall I'll be out of here, thank God. You won't catch me hanging around this house once I finish with school.

You'd think we'd get along better. We were never as bad as this before. Chris'll just never grow up. He thinks he's being funny but he's not, he's just acting like a two-year-old. And half the time he blames me for the way Dad gets. Well, that's something else. I just don't think it's fair to come home plastered every second night and I've got a right to tell him that, I don't give a damn what anybody says. It's not only *his* money he's wasting. We've got to live on it too. What kind of father gets loaded to the two eyes on Christmas Eve?

I wouldn't doubt that's half the reason Scott broke up with me — I say what's on my mind. He couldn't take the fact that he didn't get his own way all the time. He knew I was no prude but there was only so far I was willing to let him go. If that's all the reason he was going out with me for then the hell with him and I told him that. He said I was being immature and I got mad because I figured then he thought I was stupid enough to get conned into it. I said give us time and what about just love, which all sounded so phoney, but it really was what I meant. And when he said he loved me I didn't know whether or not he was telling the truth. We broke up I guess because I was confused.

But it bugs me because I like him, I still do and maybe he really did like me too. But I'm not about to go crawling back to him. That's one thing I'm not going to do.

4

CHRIS

I just got to get out of the house. I can't stick it in here any longer, not the way they're all getting on my back. A stupid present. Big deal. I'm sorry I done it, but what a thing to blow up about. I'll never understand that stupid sister of mine. She knows it was only for a joke, and I tell her that again while we're eating dinner. The look she gives me is enough to make a grizzly puke.

And that's the highlight of the meal. Dad makes it up finally, but he's too hung over to say more than two words at the table. I got to feel sorry for him just the same, because his guts must really be feeling rotten. For sure the turkey don't do anything to help matters. You need about a gallon of water to wash down every forkful of the white meat. And no dressing, and Mom knows that dressing is the best part I likes.

About one-thirty, just after we get finished with dinner, I phones up Tompkins to see what he's up to. Tompkins is the fellow I hangs around with a good bit of the time. I had a mind to phone Monica first, but probably I'll wait till later on before I do that.

The telephone cord is strung out into the hall and the door closed as much as I can get it.

"Hello, shithead, whata ya up to?"

"Sittin down, answerin the phone," he says. Tompkins can be little slack on the humour.

"Don't believe it. What else?"

"Nothin much. Guess what I got for Christmas?"

"Bo Derek?"

"Close."

"A new bra?"

"You do like takin chances with your life, don't ya?"

"What is it? Com'on, heave it outa ya."

"Come over and see."

Tompkins only lives about five minutes walk from the house. It's frosty enough outside to cut the skin off you and snowing along with that, so I'm not long getting over to his place. By the time I stops running I'm in sight of his back door. Do you know what the jerk's got parked by the steps? A brand-new Citation twin-cylinder. No kidding!

"Is that what you got for Christmas — your own skidoo?" I can hardly believe it.

"Yap."

"You mean that's all yours?"

"Well, not exactly. Shawn gets to use it sometimes, that's the deal." Shawn is his eleven-year-old brother.

"Tompkins, old man, that's not bad, not bad at all." A Citation 4500. I'm still not over it.

"Tried her yet or what?"

"Burnt up half a tank o' gas this morning."

"She got any guts?"

"Oh, she got guts all right."

"What did you get outa her?"

"I haven't had her flat out yet. Wants to break her in right."

Frig, a skidoo. Some guys are born lucky. Tompkins' old man's got a bit of dough. He's not loaded, but he must do all right working for the post office.

That afternoon he has another go at her. In fact we spend practically the whole afternoon riding around. Once we get rid of Shawn we take off up the country for about five miles. We told his father we was going to go ice fishing and we even took the ice auger to make it look good. But we're having too much fun lacin her back and forth the ponds, tearing around all over the place to go at that. She got a nice bit of guts all right. She couldn't take Bill Benson's Yamaha, but she's not bad. I wouldn't exactly turn her down if someone handed me the keys for Christmas.

The two albums I brought with me over to Tompkins' place seems pretty slack compared to what he got for Christmas, but later on we try them out on the stereo in his bedroom. His father bought a turntable and amp and speakers last year, about a thousand bucks worth of stereo equipment, and after a month it all ended up downstairs in Steve's bedroom because the music he used to play drove his parents off their head.

He's got a pretty decent record collection too. He likes a lot of the same groups I do, but what he really gets off on is Elvis Costello and The Clash. I think they're pretty good, but he freaks right out over this new wave stuff.

Tompkins' mother invites me to stay for supper. I says no first because I figure it's not very good manners to jump at the offer like you're half starved or something, but with a little coaxing she wins me over. I phones up the old lady to let her know I won't be home.

I gets along pretty good with Tompkins' parents, although his mother is not exactly a live wire when it comes to conversation. She asks at supper how my parents are and I say okay and then she gets into real lively topics like the weather and Christmas cakes — what I likes best, light fruit cakes or dark fruit cakes. She says Steven likes any kind of fruit cake. I tell her I wouldn't doubt that one bit. Tompkins wrings up a fist and starts punching it into his other hand behind his old lady's back.

I'm not the only extra one for supper, so I don't get to take part in this great discussion for long. In fact there are six others besides their own family and me — Steve's aunt and uncle and their two little kids, and another aunt who is not married, and his grandfather. That makes for eleven altogether sitting around at one big table. It's like when they advertise turkey on TV, right down to the butter oozing out when the old bird is sawed open. Piles of potatoes, cabbage, pease pudding, turnip.

For me the food is pretty much a rerun of dinner, only I ends up eating more because I'm in a better mood. There's a couple bottles of Cold Duck to wash it all down with. I have three glasses gone before I gets the feeling that Mrs. Tompkins thinks I'm hitting the bottle too hard, so I slacks off a bit. She keeps an even sharper eye on Steve. Old wino-face plays it like he's not all that fussy about the stuff. I should tell her he'd rather have a cold beer. Labatt's Blue is his brand to be exact. Tompkins would just love that.

What I really gets off on though is not the wine, but the steamed pudding she's got for dessert. Talk about something good. The rum sauce alone with the walnuts in it is enough to make your taste buds go berserk. I have three pieces. My gut is just about ready to split abroad from stuffing myself so much. When I gets up from the table I have to go to Steve's bedroom and lie down I'm so full, that's the truth.

Lying there, we try to figure out what we'll do for the rest of the night. We could maybe take the skidoo and go riding around again, only he's got to ask his father first. Tompkins always got to clear everything with his old man. His father says he already had her going all day and his mother don't like him riding around after dark. He might slam into a fence he can't see or something. It always takes a mother to come up with such a bright reason. Well, that cut out one possibility. What else? Girls, of course, although Christmas night is a rotten time to be out around because there's no place open to go. And I don't particularly enjoy freezing my arse off walking back and forth the roads.

I calls up Monica anyway. Probably you could call Monica a girlfriend. If not, she's the closest thing I got to one. I've been sorta going out with her for a few months and I likes her a fair bit. I walks her home a lot. I finds it great exercise. For my hands, that is.

"Hi, whata ya doin?"

"Watching 'Charlie Brown's Christmas' on TV." Monica can get her thrills in odd ways.

"I'm over to Tompkins' place. Goin out anywhere later on or what?"

"I don't think so."

"Why not?"

"Louise is comin over in an hour and I got to stay in after that."

"How come?"

"To baby-sit. Mom and Dad are invited out to a party."

"We'll come over and help you baby-sit." Among other things.

"Sure you will."

"Why not?"

"We're not allowed to have anyone in."

"We'll come over after the kids have gone to bed."

"No good to show up because you won't get in. All the doors'll be barred." She giggles.

"You're no fun. You two will be bored outa your minds. Whata ya goin to do for excitement —

play tiddly-winks or something?"

"Listen, I gotta go. Somebody wants to use the phone. I'll see you tomorrow, okay?"

I'm not sure if she's trying to bullshit me or not. Sometimes when you talk to Monica she can make it seem like you're the only fellow in the world she ever thinks about. More times, I don't know . . . it's like she got her mind on a million other things besides you.

"She gotta baby-sit," I tell Tompkins. "She wanted us to come over, but her old lady wouldn't hear tell of it. She's pretty mad about that."

"Sure she is."

"She is so. Can't get enough of me I spose . . . Especially certain parts." I grin.

As a matter of fact we don't end up doing much that would cause headlines — playing albums mostly and chasing Shawn and the other little torments around the bedroom. Would you believe it, we actually have a game of hide-and-seek in the basement with them just for a laugh. I can get a great kick out of little kids like that sometimes. And we must spend at least two hours playing the Electronic Quarterback game Shawn got for Christmas. We give it back to him once the battery starts getting weak.

And I have a while messing around with Tompkins' guitar. He's been teaching me a bit about playing it the last couple of months. Tompkins is pretty good. He's no Eric Clapton now but he's half decent on the acoustic he's got. That's another thing I wouldn't mind owning — a guitar. I just wish I had money enough to get one.

What I finally ends up doing is spending Christmas night at his place. He's been after me all evening to stay over and I'm not in much of a mood to be going home anyway. When I phones the house Jennifer answers. I tell her to let Mom know what I'm doing and then I gives her a fast goodbye. Before we go to bed we have a second feed because by now the turkey and pudding is wore off. Fills up this time on ice cream, with a couple of mini pizzas thrown in on the side.

I climbs inside a sleeping bag on the carpet and Tompkins uses the bed. We keep the stereo on, but turned down low because by now everybody else in the house is asleep. Sometimes, like during the summer or something when a bunch of us are camping out for the night, Tompkins and me will stay up till three and four o'clock in the morning, sometimes till daylight, just talking and telling jokes. I can't remember jokes, but Tompkins . . . he's got a memory for dirty jokes like a horny elephant. And he makes up these toilet ones that are enough to make you throw up your guts if you got a weak stomach. He should know better just the same than to think he could ever gross me out.

Eventually, like we usually do, we have a shot at talking over what girls in school would be the best to have between the sheets for a night. "I'd lay my bets on Pam Stacey," Tompkins says.

"Yeah, can't see anybody kickin her outa bed for chewin on crackers. What about Susan

Murphy in grade nine?"

"Wouldn't mind sinkin the lips into her either."

"You're not kiddin."

"Thought all you had on your mind was Monica?"

"I do . . . most times. What do you think of her?"

"Monica?"

"Yeah."

"All right I guess."

"That's all? Now what do you really think of her?"

"I dunno."

"You know but you won't say."

"She's not my type. You're the one who's goin out with her, you should know what she's like."

"Yeah, I guess I should."

5

FATHER

You got to be tough with youngsters. You can't have them telling you what to do. That's half is wrong with the world, the youngsters got it took over. I had to put the clamps on her. She's sixteen and she thinks she knows it all. And saucy along with that. And if there's one thing I'm not going to stand for it's saucy youngsters. She should a known there was only so much I could take before I put my foot down.

No, by God, she deserved it. Her mother can say what she damn well likes now, but she deserved it. I never was one for hitting youngsters, and Lucy knows that, but I wasn't about to put up with her tongue wagging in my face any longer. "Drinking again," she said, and started then to tell me off because I had a bottle of beer in my hands, as if that was any of her goddamn business. Well, I didn't raise my youngsters to poke their nose into everything I does. It was only the second beer I had for the day. And what the hell is two beer. Nothing.

Make no wonder I wouldn't have a few drinks. This place is gone to the dogs. You can't find a job that pays enough to live on. I had a job at the sawmill and they had to close it down because they couldn't get anybody who had sense enough to run it right. Then when you goes to build something the only half-decent lumber you can get your hands on is what they trucks in from the mainland. And our own timber then rotting away in the woods. The government should have its ass kicked.

I got laid off in October and you think I can get something to work at. No goddamn way. Sit around all day drawing unemployment, waiting for someone to come up with a Canada Works Grant or some goddamn thing. And what do they pay you then — the minimum wage. The government expects a man to look after a wife and two youngsters on the minimum wage, with the prices the way they are today. Make no wonder I wouldn't drink.

Draw unemployment if there's no work or go off to Alberta or Toronto some place and look for a job. That or go on the dole, and that's one thing I won't be doing, that's for damn well sure. Father never done it and he seen some worse times than what I have. How many people is sponging off the government because they're too bloody lazy to go look for a job. Bad backs they says. Some goddamn bad backs I knows.

Well sir, if it comes to that I'll pack up and take off to Alberta. I got a first cousin out there now and he's doing all right for hesself. He's a foreman and he can get me a job no sweat. I don't want to leave, and Luce and Chris sure don't. But what can I do. If I had money enough and there was any way I could make a living at it, I'd get a long liner and go fishing. There's talk of someone putting a fish plant here, but you mightn't see that for the next ten years. I gets sick altogether of lying around with nothing to do. Give me another few months and if nothing turns up by that time, I'm taking off. Leave Lucy and the kids here and see if I can't get a job in Alberta.

Meanwhile, so I haves a few drinks. So I plays a few games of darts in the club. There's frig all else to do. Today is St. Stephen's Day. There'll be a good booze out of this yet. Before long the boys'll be showing up here like they always do for a drink and I spose we'll go off and make the rounds. I'm not passing up a few drinks on St. Stephen's Day. Christmas just wouldn't be Christmas if I did.

CHRIS

By the time I gets around to leaving Tompkins' place it's two o'clock in the afternoon. I walks for about fifteen minutes to get to Monica's. It turns out that she's not home and her mother says she haven't got a clue where she might be to. I guess she's out looking for me.

I don't come across her anywhere. And it's four o'clock or later before I gives it up and walks home.

When I gets in the house the kitchen is filled up with men. There's a 40-ouncer of Captain

Morgan on the table, still three parts full, and a roaster of leftover turkey that half the crowd is picking through to find something they can chew on. I knows every one of them, they're all from around the place, just starting out making their Boxing Day rounds. Ours is usually one of the first places where they show up.

A few of them are well on already. They must a got a head start on the crowd because they usually have only one drink to a house. They'll stay in each place about ten minutes and then they're gone. Whatever man is in the house who wants to go is gone with them, till by eight or nine o'clock in the night there might be two dozen or more in the crowd, those that can still walk. Most times it's a great laugh because you always get two or three comical fellows in amongst the bunch and perhaps some fellow with a mouth organ or an accordion.

Mom is fairly good about it all, I suppose. I figured after yesterday she'd still be half dirty. Course you can't have a sour face with that bunch and expect to get away with it. After all it's Christmas, and Boxing Day boozers have been on the go as long as I can remember. It hardly seems the same as it's been some years though. I can remember when she'd have stuff cooked purpose for when they'd show up and be the one to start someone singing, more than just being there stood up by the kitchen sink. Somehow I thinks the men take notice of that too.

Soon someone is yelling that it's about time they got a move on and they'll never make it to all the houses they got in mind to go to if they don't get going. They trail off out the door and of course Dad is right tight behind them.

"Gord, now watch where you're goin. I half expects to get a call one of these times that you've been struck by a car or something."

"Don't worry."

"Now you're not going without something on your head. You'll have pneumonia the next thing."

"Hurry up and find something then." He seems willing to come back in the kitchen and wait. Probably he expected her to try and talk him outa going.

He looks at me, who's the only one left in the kitchen besides himself. "Where ya been to Chris?" he says.

"Ah, nowhere much."

"You and Steve out chasing after the girls again I spose."

I grin. "Mom," I yells down the hall, "anybody phone, lookin for me?"

"No," she calls back.

"I knew it," he says. "I don't know what in the world they sees in you fellows."

"Must be our good looks," I tell him, stroking my chin and clearing my throat.

He starts to laugh.

"Guess what?"

"What?"

"Steve's old man got him a new skidoo for Christmas."

"That right?"

"Yeah."

"That's pretty good."

"Yeah."

He don't say anymore about it, so I ask him, "What about the skidoo you said we might get, that second-hand one off Wilf Drover?"

"Wants too much for her."

"How much?"

"Five hundred bucks."

"She's in good shape though," I tell him.

"No odds. If we haven't got the money, we haven't got the money."

"Perhaps you can talk him down."

"We'll see. Luce, hurry up with that cap. They're halfway up the road by now."

That means he's not even going to try. "Another winter and no skidoo."

"Now Chris, don't start keepin on about skidoos again. I had enough of that last winter."

Mom comes back in the kitchen with a cap for him, Jennifer behind her. Dad seems surprised that she's there. She looks more crabby than usual because her face is like it's swollen up or something. I can't tell very good because she has make-up plastered all over it.

"What's the matter now?" Mom says.

"Goddamn skidoos again, you might know."

"I only asked," I tell him. "I only asked."

Then Jennifer's big mouth cuts in. "What, you mean dear little Chris didn't get his own way for once?"

"Now don't *you* start again," Mom warns her.

She gets in front of the old man and practically pushes him through the kitchen door. "Now go on."

But he moves her to one side with his arm and forces his way back in.

"And what do you mean by that?" he asks Jennifer.

"Just what I said."

"Now young lady, don't go gettin snotty wit me. If you didn't learn a good lesson out of the crack I give you this mornin, then I got another one that just might do the trick."

"Gord, I said go on if you're goin. A minute ago you was tearin your ass to pieces to get out. Now go on!"

She tries to get him back out in the porch. He goes, but it's only after he sees that Jennifer is not about to open her mouth again. After he leaves the house Mom shuts the outside door and then comes in and closes the kitchen door.

"The frigger," Jennifer says.

"Now Jennifer."

"I hope to God he comes home so drunk he doesn't regain consciousness for a week."

"Jennifer! Now hold your tongue."

"What's eatin her?"

Neither one of them will answer me.

"What happened? . . . He didn't really hit her, did he?"

"Chris, it's none of your concern."

Nobody will say anything. I don't really believe that he would hit her. But her face *is* swollen up.

"Yes, he hit me. Now are you satisfied?"

"How come ?"

"Because he's retarded, that's how come."

"Jennifer, shut up!" Mom says. "If you didn't always have your tongue goin he mightn't a got mad."

"Now you're takin his side, I suppose."

"I'm not takin anybody's side. Forget about it. That's all you got to do. Forget about it."

"Forget about it! Sure!"

"I'm not arguing with you, so don't start. I've had enough of this for one day. Now I don't want to hear another word about it." Mom goes to the closet and hauls out the vacuum cleaner and drags it into the living room. Once she sets it going the sound it makes puts a dull roar over everything.

I never knowed him to get that mad with her. I can't think that he would go that far, not Dad. Frig, I don't know. He's been so touchy here lately, he's liable to do anything. But it's hard to think just the same that he would haul off and smack Jennifer in the side of the face. He's pretty sick if he did do it.

Shit, I don't know what it is with the old man. Just being in the house now is enough to get on your nerves.

MOTHER

There was a time when there was twice this much mess in the house at Christmas and I wouldn't mind cleaning it up half so much. You wouldn't have carpet on the living-room floor then either. It was harder work. If Jennifer had to do today what my mother had me do then she wouldn't have the time to be getting into the scrape that she got into. Not that I owes one bit with what Gord done, but that's half the trouble — she's got too much time to just lie around the house.

I wish sometimes there was no such a thing as Christmas. That's an awful thing to be saying, but God knows it was never meant to be like it is now. One big excuse to spend money and get drunk, that's all it amounts to. And the youngsters then, they're not satisfied with anything unless it got a two-hundred-dollar price tag on it. Sometimes I feels like stuffing the Christmas tree and the whole damn lot into the garbage can.

One time sure if you got a new pair of mitts and a few candies you'd be satisfied. You had to be satisfied. That's all there was to get. If your father had the time to make you a cradle for your doll or something, well, my God, you thought you had your fortune. You wouldn't sleep for a week. Now half the families is till August month paying off what they had for their youngsters for Christmas. No way is we going at that.

I'm sick and tired of it. I longs for Christmas to be over and for the two of them to be back to school, that's the god's truth. For sure tonight'll be another two o'clock job. Somebody'll dump him off on the doorstep, boozed up again. It's getting so that I don't give a damn half the time what happens to him. It's shockin, he's worse now than ever he was.

I don't mind anybody taking a few drinks. You wouldn't survive in this world if you was like that. But there's so much liquor on the go now see they don't know when to stop. One time each family'd have a couple of bottles and that'd last all during Christmas. Now they're not satisfied if they don't see the bottom of the bottle once it's put on the table.

6

CHRIS

January came and went without a skidoo. So did February. By that time I had given up on it anyway and the word never was mentioned in the house for the rest of the winter. Tompkins let me drive his a good many times, but it's nowheres near as good as having one of your own to fool around with.

And just guess what the old man went and done this week? He sold the car.

It was five years old and not in very good shape but at least it was a set of wheels around the place. He said we needed the money. More booze money I wouldn't doubt. I suppose now when I gets old enough to get my licence there won't be a lousy thing for me to drive. I've been counting the days for the past six years till the time I can write my beginners. I can drive now probably as good as I'll ever be able to seeing that I've been practising for so long. Frig it, I put up with not having a skidoo, I'm going to have a car or something even if I got to quit school and go find a job.

I'm not spending much time in the house

these days. There's no sense to it. There's hardly two words said but somebody gets into a racket. About the only fun I've had in the last few weeks has been with Tompkins. And Norm, Tompkins' father.

We went out last Saturday turr hunting. We did all right too, come back with three and a half dozen birds between the three of us. That was the first time I ever was out like that after turrs. I'd planned on going out with the old man this winter but, of course, we never did get around to it. That Saturday was pretty good fun though. We struck on a good day — cold, but sunny and hardly any sea on. We didn't think we was going to have much luck first, but by seven o'clock or so we struck into them. Norm said it was one of the thickest times he's ever seen turrs. He got me to look out to the motor so him and Steve could have a try at them.

After Steve killed a half dozen or so, then he took the motor and handed me over his gun. There was a few birds pretty close to the boat at the time, but I must a been shooting too high first because I missed them altogether. After I got used to the gun I made out all right though. I'd say five birds was pretty decent for my first time at it. I knows one thing — it looked good seeing Tompkins' old man haul them aboard the boat in the dip net.

We was back in again by ten o'clock. Norm thought we might have a chance at a seal, but we wasn't lucky enough to see either one. We went to work that same morning and picked all the turrs. And had six of them for supper that night. Tompkins' old lady is not easy when it comes to putting a good flavour on turrs.

All in all it was about the best bit of fun I've had lately. That and going in the woods. Me and Tompkins have started spending a lot of time in the woods after school, cutting birch. We must a cut 150 turn or more and hauled them out by skidoo. I'd say we should make a fair bit of money off it too, once we gets it all cut up and sold. We already got over half of it bargained for.

I could use a bit of extra money to cheer me up, with all the other things that's bugging me. One of them is my marks at school. They're not exactly much to cheer about these days.

Another is Monica. It happened last Friday night, at the teenage dance in the Legion. I'd been there a full friggin hour waiting for her before she even showed up.

"Where you been all this time?" I said when she finally come in through the door.

"Baby-sitting. Mom only just got home."

"How come you never let me know you had to baby-sit?"

"I didn't know myself till I started to get ready for the dance. And I can't stay for long. She's got to go out again in half an hour."

"Shit on that."

"No good gettin mad about it. You want to dance or what?"

"I dunno."

After a few minutes she had me bugged enough that I got out on the floor. I didn't have much of a mind for it first, but she soon started to do a few things to change that. Like dancing closer during the slow one than she ever did before. And kissing me on the neck. And then long and hard on the mouth. Made me wonder what she could think up for an encore.

"I better go," she said then, after only three or four songs.

"It's not a half hour yet."

"By the time I gets home it will be."

"I'll walk you home."

"Naw, that's okay. You can stay here. I wouldn't doubt Mom'll be at the front door waitin for me. I'll see you tomorrow." She kissed me again.

So I let her go on. And all I did for the next ten minutes then was sit there. Like some dummy.

See, unless you got a few beer in you or something, it's the shits altogether not having some girl to hang around with when you're at a dance. Makes me think I looks queer or something just sitting there alone. It's okay if there's a bunch standing around talking. But when everybody pairs off and you get left there by yourself it can make you feel like a fool. That or you end up dancing with some broad who was left over and looks like a reject from plastic surgery.

About the only thing I got out of sitting there like that was the chance to have a good long look at Susan Murphy. I couldn't keep my eyes off her. She was out on the floor dancing with her boyfriend. I can't see what the hell she sees in that guy.

Even when I got up to go outside she was on my mind. I figured the best thing I could do was to hunt down a few of the boys and see if there was any beer on the go. I took a look out back of the Legion, but there wasn't anybody around, except for a few people necking. Maybe they was in one of the cars parked in the field across the road.

The only car that seemed to have anybody in it was Len Ivany's. Perhaps he knew where they was to. I went over and knocked on the window.

I started to knock again when all of a sudden I saw the reason he wasn't too quick to roll it down. The baby-sitter herself was in the car — Monica.

He looked at me. "How ya doin, Chris?"

"Never mind." I turned around and started back across the road.

"He's just givin me a drive back home," I heard Monica say.

Just how friggin dumb did she think I was. Baby-sitting. Baby-sitting my ass. The old bat, she can get her thrills from someone who's more sucker than I am. I hope her cans shrink up.

Frig it, I never cared much about her anyway. I might have one time, but I sure as hell don't anymore. And I didn't only go after her for the bit of a feel I got now and then. Although I suppose you got to find something more exciting than cranking yourself.

The truth of it all is I would a dropped that jerk of a Monica long ago if I thought I had chance to get out with someone like Susan Murphy. Too bad she goes out with that twit she's got for a boyfriend. I bet you half the reason she goes out with him is because he's got a motorcycle. It might seem stupid but Susan Murphy drives me crazy. I mean there are others who are probably better built, but there's just something about her that drives me crazy. It's the way she jokes around or something. She laughs a lot but she's not loud or anything. There's just something about her.

Every night since that dance I've been wanting to call her up, except that I figure I'll probably make a fool of myself doing it. I'm okay once I knows a girl pretty good and I've been out with her a few times and then I calls her up, but to phone up someone you hardly ever spoke to before, especially if you like her a lot . . . well I might just come off sounding like an idiot.

Tompkins says what the hell, I'm not going to get anywhere just thinking about it. Anyway all I wants to do is talk to her, sorta give her a hint I likes her.

I starts off cool enough. "Hi. This is Chris. I just made five bucks off this phone call."

"Chris who?"

Chris who? Well, shit.

"Chris Slade. You know Steve Tompkins, right? He said he'd give me five bucks if I'd call you up."

He didn't really but I thought it was a good way to start. We got something to talk about right away instead of ah this or ah that, right?

"What's wrong, has he got arthritis?"

See what I mean about her sense of humour. If that was Monica she would probably just giggle like some numbskull.

"He didn't have to call you, *I* did. He *bet* me five bucks."

"That's a good way to make money. What is he — a bank vault?"

"He's got loads of money. He hires himself out nights."

Here she laughs and Steve, who's standing up next to me, hauls off with the back of his hand and whacks me in the nuts. Frig, talk about a pain. I takes a swipe at him with the phone.

"Are you goin to the next dance?" I grunt, still half bent over.

"Probably."

"I'll probably see you there."

Then the silence starts. She was supposed to say okay or something like that. But all I hears is this deadness on the line, like she's just booted the phone into outer space or something.

"Do you like goin to those dances?"

"They're okay."

Silence.

"Yeah, they're okay." More silence. "Doin much work at school?"

"I have a test tomorrow."

"Oh."

So much for the terrific little questions.

"Well, I guess I better go," I say.

"Okay."

Shit, what is that supposed to mean — okay.

"See ya."

"Goodbye."

See what I mean about fooling things up.

I've been wanting to phone her back ever since. But what's the point when old leatherhead is dragging her around on a motorcycle half the time. Sometimes I'd like to plant a bomb in that stupid helmet he wears. Give him something to put his brains in order.

See if I had something to drive I'd be okay. I can't wait to get my licence. And a car or a motorcycle. I don't care what kind, just so long as it's got a bit of power. Mom goes right off the head when I tell her I'm getting a motorcycle this summer if I can land a job. All she talks about is what would happen if I had an accident. I knows there's lots of accidents with cycles. But what odds, I'll be careful. A cycle is a friggin nice thing to have.

I knows what half of it is — Mom is still dirty with me because I quit being a server. I just couldn't hack it anymore. I still goes to church now and then when she can get me outa bed. But I just couldn't take all that any longer. And I told her it was no good for her to try to talk me out of it. I got my own mind to make up. Dad couldn't very well say much seeing he haven't been to church since November.

Tompkins didn't think much of the way I quit. But who cares. Tompkins haven't got guts enough to quit. He's scared of what his old lady'd say. She might just get it in her head to sell the skidoo or something.

Actually it wasn't either one of them that I was thinking about the most, it was Rev. Wheaton. See Rev. Wheaton has always been pretty good to me. We've always got along real good as a matter of fact. He's not at all what you'd picture most ministers to be like. He's not high and mighty or he don't go around rubbing your hair like you're six years old. I mean he talks to you like you're fifteen, not a youngster. He jokes and carries on a lot, but he can be serious too when he gets it in his head. I mean he's pretty decent. He got me going on this serving business and I must say it was okay while I was at it. In fact I sorta enjoyed it. It was something of a club — we'd get together and play sports sometimes and go on trips together. Plus it was Rev. Wheaton who got me started going to summer camp. The church has these ten-day camps every summer near Ochre Pond. It's a good bit of fun. Tompkins and me have gone there three years in a row. In fact we're supposed to be going back there this summer as counsellors, at least we gave Rev. Wheaton our names last summer so we could go.

The camp is not a holy, holy place. You don't have hymns coming out of the trees or anything. I mean there's a bit of religion. You can't very well not have some religion at a church camp, but, I don't know, you don't notice it. It just fits in as part of everything else that goes on. There's a lot of sports and campfires and skits and a bit of a wild time. What I likes about it most is you get to meet all kinds of people from all over the place.

Anyway it was Wheaton who got me started going there. So I hated to tell him I was quit being a server. But I had to quit. After all I'm almost sixteen. I got too much other stuff on my mind. I got Tompkins to give him the message. I didn't feel like telling him face-to-face because I knows he'd only try to get me to change my mind. I wouldn't doubt, though, it's frigged up my chances of getting to Ochre Pond as a counsellor. That's what I'm thinking about the most.

7

FATHER

Finally, after three trips into Bakerton, I got the stupid ticket straightened out with Manpower. Some of the people the government's got working for them, I don't think they knows what they're doing half the time. They're paying my way up to Calgary and it took three trips into their office now to get it fixed up. I'm leaving this Saturday. I can't stick it any longer around here with no job. I thought I might have a chance to get on with Atlantic Construction at the road work they're doing, but I never got no satisfaction out of that. There's too many fellows after the same jobs. Once I found that out, I phoned Ches in Calgary right away and now he's got a job lined up for me. I'm not thinking about moving the family yet. I've got to see how well I likes it before I even considers that. I might be back on the plane again in two weeks if it don't work out no sense.

Luce and the two youngsters came with me to the airport. And Jack, from next door, it's hes car we drove in. He'll take them back home once the plane gets off the ground. I don't feel the best about leaving the family. But what choice have I got. It's either that or starve. Jennifer and Chris should be old enough to take care of themselves, that's one good thing. It's not like I was leaving her with two small youngsters to look after. She should be able to manage all right. I told her to make them help her out around the house.

I had a talk with Chris before I left home. Another three weeks and he'll be out of school. Now, I said, you look for a job once school is over. He'll put his name in at Manpower, but I doubt if that's going to do him much good. Have a good look around and try to come up with something to do for the summer, I told him. Even if it is only three or four weeks' work.

I'd say the same to Jennifer only she don't heed me anymore. She wants to go to university in the fall. It's an awful lot of money to send a youngster to university. I can't see how we can afford it. If I can stick with a half-decent job, then maybe. If not she'll have to go look for a student loan, that's all I can tell her. And if that's not enough, well, she'll just have to work for a year and save her money.

She don't say much when we're all sitting down there in the terminal waiting for them to announce the flight. She don't look at me, she's more interested in watching all the people walking back and forth. Chris spends a while fooling around at a car game or something, but then he comes over and sits down alongside of me.

"Remember what I told you about lookin for a job."

"Yeah."

"Stay out of trouble. And do what your mother says."

"Okay, okay. When do you figure you'll be back?"

"I can't say. Could be two weeks, could be two months, could be ten months. It all depends whether I likes it up there or not."

"I hope we don't have to move." He screws up his face. "Maybe there'll be something come up around here by then."

"Maybe."

Luce is trying to fix up the collar on my windbreaker. I can't stand to have women fooling around at my clothes like that.

"I only wants you to look a bit tidy. If you hadn't put so much weight on your stomach your clothes would fit you better. You're not flying across Canada lookin like some tramp. Now have you got it straight about where you changes planes?"

"Montreal, it's written on the ticket."

"Now if you can't find your way around, ask somebody."

"Luce, I'll get there, don't worry about it."

"I knows it's not the first time you've been on a plane. I'm just thinkin something might happen. Now call us as soon as you gets there, remember that. I don't care what time of the night it is."

The Air Canada speaker comes on then, and it's time for me to get checked through. Luce wants me to sit down for a few minutes longer but

I figure it's just as well to go and get it over with. They comes along with me to the line-up at the security gate, all except Jennifer. I gives Luce a kiss. It's only then that it dawns on me that this will be the first time in a dozen years or more that we'll be away from each other for very long. Ever since I worked that year in Labrador.

I puts my arm on Chris's shoulder and tells him to make sure he behaves himself and from that then I walks over to where Jennifer is standing up so I can tell her goodbye. She says goodbye and I kisses her on the cheek.

"I hope you does good in your exams . . . I mean you'll do good anyway . . ."

She won't even bring herself to look at me right.

When I gets back in the line-up there's only three people ahead of me, so I tells Luce and Chris that they better go on.

The goddamn foolish thing is that once the overnight bag I got in my hand goes along the conveyor belt, the stupid girl on the other side wants me to open up the parcel that's inside.

"It's only a few lobsters and a few tins of moose meat." It's a parcel Ches's mother give me to carry up to him.

"I'm sorry sir, I have to go by the regulations."

The damn regulations, and when I goes aboard the plane I still can't get the parcel to fit back right into the overnight bag. The zipper won't do up. I gives it a shove in under the seat so I can have a cigarette and try to calm down a bit before they switches on the no smoking sign. I never did like it in an airplane. It makes me feel too cramped up.

CHRIS

I miss the old man a good bit. I didn't really like to see him go. If it wasn't for not having to listen to him rowing with everybody I guess I'd miss him a lot more.

The last day of school was yesterday. When it was over I took my time coming home. I was trying to figure out how I was going to face the old lady with all the lousy marks I got.

I flunked grade ten. My life has just been too cheerful here lately. Man, I'm soon going to need to take lessons in how to get depressed.

I felt pretty stupid being one of only two people in the class who flunked, but what odds. What's done is done. Up to Christmas I was doing pretty good. I was passing at least. I dunno, I slacked off too much I guess. I tried to do some work during the last week when we had the exams but even then I couldn't seem to get at it. Especially with the warm weather we was having and the long days. Half of what you do in school anyway is a pile of crap. What good is it to you once you get out? If you got a job as a mechanic or welder or something who's going to be asking you about the Treaty of Versailles or junk like that? Who's going to need to know how to factorize a stupid equation so they can change a set of spark plugs?

I knows that don't sound like much of an excuse. I should a been working all year if I expected to pass. I knows that. One time I could scrape by without studying at all, but I guess when you're in high school it don't come so easy as that anymore. But I don't give a shit. School is over for the year. The way I'm feeling now I might never go back.

Mom got to see the report card after a while. I left it lying on the kitchen table so when she got home she'd have a little something to read in case she was bored out of her mind with nothing to do. I don't see her until I gets up at 11 o'clock this morning. By now she pretty well has the whole thing memorized, right down to the last of the wonderful details — 4 F's, 2 D's, and a C. At least I was fairly consistent.

She's in no mood for jokes. I can't say actually that I expect her to be.

"Now don't go yellin at me," I tell her. "I flunked and that's it." I'm in no mood for a lecture.

She don't buy that so quick. "Well, don't think you're going to get off that easy. How in the world could you ever do so bad?"

"It wasn't easy."

"Now don't try to be funny about it! You didn't pass all the years you been in school and fail this time for no reason."

"Blame it on the teachers."

"You don't blame the teachers for 4 F's. That's stupid."

"Okay, so I'm stupid. So now you got your reason."

"Chris, stop it! What's got into you for God's sake? When you was in the elementary grades you done all right all the way up through. But since you got into high school you've got worse and worse. But you never done this bad before. Last year you never got all that good o' marks but you passed every subject."

"So I flunked one year. So what? It's the first time."

"But there was no need of it if you'd a studied."

"I hates studying."

"I can see that by these marks. You just got to learn to like it. It's not goin to kill ya. What about Jennifer? She studies and gets good marks. Why in the world can't you be more like that?"

"Because I'm not like her that's why and I don't want to be."

By this time I'm halfway out the door.

"And where do you think you're goin?"

"To look for a job," I yell at her.

"Be back in the house for dinner."

I don't answer. If she wants another Jennifer she's just going to have to find someone else besides me. What she said pisses me off for the whole rest of the day. So what if I flunked grade ten. There's nothing anybody can do about it now.

63

MOTHER

I don't know what to do with him. He's fifteen, almost sixteen. You can't lace him and send him off to bed anymore.

See Gord is half the reason he gets like that. He was never stubborn like that when he was younger. You could talk to him, reason with him. Now he's getting so he thinks he knows it all.

You can't make youngsters study. You can only tell them so many times and then what are you supposed to do. They gets the opportunity to go to school and they'd just as soon beat the streets all day. They don't know how lucky they are. When I was fifteen I had to give up school and go out to work. And now it breaks my heart to see him just throw it all away.

I don't know . . . if the teachers was stricter then maybe this never would a happened. The students today gets away with too much, to my mind. There's no such thing as discipline anymore, not like what it was when I was going to school. At least we learned a few manners.

What do you do? Leave him alone I suppose and perhaps he'll learn. If he spends a few weeks doing some labour work he'll soon change his tune. I hope to God he do get something to work at so that his summer won't all be a waste.

I'm that tired myself now by the time I gets home in the night that I'm ready to flop right in the bed. With Gord gone there's not so much to do around the house. That's one reason I did what

I did. I took a job for the summer.

It's odd when you thinks about the way Gord was tearing himself to pieces to try and come up with something to do, and here I'm the one who's gone out to work. It don't pay a big lot and it's only for the summer. All it is is cooking at a take-out place. It's Jack's brother, Frank, who runs it, and I'm doubtful if I would a got the job except for that. Frank, though, is the nicest kind of person to be working for.

It's not myself I done it for mostly. Jennifer wants to go to university in September and if there's any way to do it I'm going to see that she gets there. I never had chance for anything like that myself, but she's not going to miss out. I don't know how much we can depend on what Gord is making for that, so if I can put aside so much from my cheque each week then that'll be a help. Jennifer's been after me for a long time to get a job, not so's she could have the money now, but because she said it'd do me good to get out of the house. After seventeen years, housework all day long is enough to get anybody down. Now I wouldn't do it while the children was small, because I don't believe in having a baby-sitter raise your youngsters, but now that they've got older I think it's only right I should get out more.

The only thing I thinks about is Chris in the house alone. I'm worried that he's going to leave on the stove or something and catch the house afire. I wouldn't mind if it was only Jennifer because she knows how to look out to things, but

Chris is just as liable to go off and leave something frying on the stove as anything. I put up a sign in the kitchen and told him a thousand times about it so perhaps he'll take notice.

I don't like leaving him to look out to himself like this, but he should be old enough now. He's gone half the time out of the house anyway and he's got his own key. I'd hardly be able to keep track of him even if I was there all day, cause when they gets that old there's no way to keep eyes on them all the time. I trusts him not to get into trouble. I just hope now he can come up with a job for the summer. But he's going back to do his grade ten over, supposing I got to drive him there with a stick.

8

CHRIS

To make things worse I haven't got no job out of it yet. That's going to make summer some friggin boring. I tried every place that I thought I might get on and they didn't have no work or they hired someone older than me. To tell you the truth, what I'd like to have is a job at a gas station. That's a good job for a fellow for the summer. But you know what they went and hired at the Ultramar station — two girls, neither one of who can tell the difference between a gas cap and a headlight, they're that stun about cars. I know — Jennifer is one of them, the big jerk. Okay, so she needs the money for next year, but it'd be all right if I had a few bucks of my own too. I wants to get a cycle.

And another thing that friggin bugs me is that Tompkins got a job out of it too. It wasn't Tompkins himself though that got the job, it was his old man got it for him. See it's not *what* you know, it's *who* you know. It's going to last him almost all summer. His old man is friends with the fellow who runs the Riverview Motel. He goes moose hunting with him every fall or something and he got him hired on.

That leaves me nowhere. Lying around the house all summer — that's something to look forward to, I know. When a fellow gets fifteen he needs to have a job for the summer. He wants something to do with his time to make a bit of money. I wouldn't give a frig if it is only digging ditches as long as I was getting paid for it.

The Friday night after the summer holidays started me and Tompkins and another fellow, Rideout, got underway for a bloody good tear. I had to do something to take my mind off things. We scraped up enough money for a dozen Labatt's Blue and a dozen Black Horse between the three of us. Terry, Tompkins' cousin, gets it for us any time we wants it. All we got to do is track him down. I don't have a hell of a lot to celebrate, but just getting out of school is reason enough to get on the beer. Terry drops us off by the woods and then takes off again with his girlfriend. That girlfriend he got is quite the piece of gear. We offer him a few bottles for getting it for us but he won't take them. No doubt he's got a lot more interesting things than beer on his mind.

I hardly used to drink much at all until last summer. And I didn't go drinking all that often this year, except on weekends. Even when I did go on the beer I made sure not to get real drunk, because I knew if I got sick as bad as I was there last year I'd be kicking myself for weeks. One time towards the end of last summer we got on it — the first time I ever had so much I didn't know what the frig I was doing. I chugged three or four beer in about twenty minutes and then I started in on the hard liquor. I must a put away three parts of a flask of vodka myself. That's all I remember. I passed out and the boys dragged me back to the tent somehow. Fierce. Lucky thing we was sleeping out that night or I might a got into some real shit. I threw up all over the sleeping bag as it was, and I had a hangover then the next day enough to kill an ox. I made a vow that I'd never get that friggin drunk again.

Most times I was pretty careful. I wouldn't want the old lady to catch me. I don't really know if she figures I drinks or not. I guess she must think I have a scattered one. I can't see anything wrong with having a few beer. Me and Tompkins only goes on it when we don't have any school the next day, and we try to stay clear of the dope. Not saying now we haven't toked up a few times when there's been any good stuff on the go. But good weed is not always easy to come by. Besides, you'd almost want to be a millionaire to keep yourself going around here.

Generally it's beer. A good booze can be a great laugh and besides, there's frig all else to do most weekends. I'll go to a movie now and then when there's anything good on, or to a dance. I can go to a dance and not drink much especially if I've got myself latched on to some girl. Course now I haven't got that to worry about either.

Where we go drinking is mostly down by the beach. It's a good place because there's no one to bother you. Tonight is the most I guess I ever seen here. Everybody's got the same idea — a good tear now that we're out of school. There's plenty of girls around. Of course a booze is no friggin good unless there's a few girls to liven things up.

It all turns out to be a real laugh, especially after the first dozen and a half are gone. Six beer each mightn't sound like many, but when I'm drinking them one right after another like tonight, and nothing to eat or anything, it's not long before I starts feeling it.

Monica is there around the beach somewhere. I seen her come down. She knows better, though, than to come around where I'm to. Give her ten minutes and someone'll probably have her laid out in the trees anyway, I wouldn't doubt. Maureen and Lorna are not exactly the best-looking broads in the world, but they'll do for a laugh. I'm not about to put the makes on either one of them so it's no trouble to overlook the missing teeth and the 12-inch scars. The best thing about them is that they're pretty good friends with Susan. I ask them where she is and they don't seem to know, except they figure she'll be around sometime. With leatherhead in tow, no doubt.

She shows up not fifteen minutes after I say that. She comes down the path slow, stopping and looking around. She's wearing a pair of those baggy pants and sort of a loose top with a belt. She's got a grey sweater hanging around her shoulders, with the arms tied in front. It don't do much for her figure but I've got that memorized anyway. Once she spies Maureen and Lorna, she wanders over and stands up near us, her hands in her pockets.

"Have you guys seen Jeff around anywhere? He was supposed to meet me here."

Might a known what she's looking for. What, has old zipper-brain gone and lost himself again?

"No," Maureen tells her.

"Haven't seen his motorcycle either."

Perhaps he got lucky and blew a valve.

"Sit down for a few minutes."

"Yeah, we won't bite," I tell her.

"Only nibble."

Just too funny, Tompkins. The boy's mind must be working overtime.

"Chris, tell her the joke you just told us."

Tompkins, I'm thinking, will you shut up. "No way."

"Rideout, you tell it." Tompkins says.

"Rideout, knock off." It's one of the grossest jokes you ever heard. It wouldn't exactly do much for my image. "She don't want to hear that."

"Tell it anyway."

I can't very well stop him. That would make it pretty obvious what I thinks of her.

"Gross!" she says when Rideout finishes, and doesn't laugh.

"Oh well, so much for that. Slade, I thought you said she had a sense of humour?"

"I didn't say that."

"Yes, you did. Slade here's got a head right full of details about you."

I'd like to clave that Rideout. He's got a friggin mouth on him big enough to drive a tractor trailer through.

"That's nice," she says. "At least one of you fellows is putting your brain to good use." She smiles.

Excellent. That shut him up pretty fast. And the way she said it, it didn't come out like she's trying to be a snob or anything.

"Shot down, Rideout." I love it.

Then the conversation slacks off into talk about how good it is to be out of school for the summer. That's okay, but after a while they get around to talking about marks and going into another grade next year and of course I don't fit in so friggin good when it comes to that.

"I don't care anyway," I says. "I don't give a frig about school."

When I looks at Susan I can see that what I said don't do much to impress her. Now I'm feeling like someone with the intelligence of a cockroach.

Then Rideout and Tompkins come up with the bright idea of getting the other two girls to go for a walk partway along the beach, leaving me and Susan by ourselves. Her to look out for her boyfriend, me to make a fool of myself again. See by this time I'm pretty well on. Frig, I'd give my right nut most times to be alone with her, but not when I'm feeling drunk. I'm half afraid to open my mouth, afraid she'll think even less of me than she already does.

What I says to her is, "I'm not as dumb as you might think," which seemed okay when I thought of it, but which probably comes out sounding like just that — dumb.

"Oh, I don't think you're dumb," she says.

"Thanks."

"Just drunk."

She keeps looking around like she's uncomfortable. She's looking for leatherhead no doubt.

"It's too bad I'm drunk."

"Why?"

"Because I'd like to talk to you, sensible."

"What about?"

"I can't say."

"Why not?"

"It mightn't come out right."

"Say it anyway. I won't laugh." She's serious.

"I'd like to go out with you."

There, that's it. I would never have opened my face like that if I'd been sober. My tongue would probably be jammed solid on the roof of my mouth or something. But you know the way it is when you're half-cut. The thing is, she's half embarrassed from what I can tell.

"I mean I knows you're already going with old leatherhead." Shit! I must be drunk.

"What?"

"I mean Jeff, you're still going with him."

"He's a nice guy."

"You could do worse."

"What do you mean?"

"Me." Shit, I don't know what the frig I'm saying.

"You're drunk."

"Yeah, you could be right. Let's forget it."

"Forget what?"

"What I said."

"That you want to go out with me."

"No!"

She laughs then and I realize she's only fooling around. It's such a friggin nice laugh. I gets right off on the way she laughs. When she does it I feels a sudden urge to put my arms around her and squeeze into her. And frig, then I go over and try to do it. Like I said, booze gives you the nerve.

She gets half mad at that. All I wanted to do was show her how I felt about how she laughed and how good it was. That's all. But what I done was frig things up. As usual.

What messes things up altogether is the sound of leatherhead's cycle coming down the path. She gets up really quick. I mean she could a got up quick, but there was no need to try to break the world record for the hundred-yard dash getting away from me before his headlights shine our way. Things like that don't do a hell of a lot to boost a fellow's ego.

Jeff parks the motorcycle at the end of the path and the two of them go off somewhere walking. I hope he trips and breaks a leg. I stays there where I've been all night, by myself with a half dozen beer still in the case. I lowers down two more before Tompkins shows up again.

"Where's the girls? And Rideout?"

"I dunno. Gone off somewhere. Rideout said not to drink his beer, he'll be back sometime. I came back to see how you made out with Susan. Leatherhead showed up, did he?"

"You might know."

"So much for that."

"I feels like gettin fuckin polluted," I says to him.

"Knock off," Tompkins says, "you got eight or nine beer gone now and we got to get home yet tonight. I got to be in by twelve and I wants to leave some time to sober up a bit."

"You goin to drink the two more you owns?"

"Naw, not tonight. I don't want to chance it. Hide em away till tomorrow night."

"Give em to me, I'll drink em."

"You won't make it home."

"Frig off, I will. As long as I'm in the house before she gets off work, the old lady'll never know." I've got the cap off one of them before he can say anything. "Com'on, drink the other beer. You're soft."

"I don't want it."

"Com'on, it's only one more. So what if they smells beer on ya?"

"So *what*? I won't get out for a week."

"Tompkins, you know what?"

"What?"

"I'm fuckin drunk."

"You're tellin me."

I don't remember everything after that. I remember I was going to drink the other beer too only Tompkins hid it away on me. And I remember trying to piss all over leatherhead's motorcycle, only Tompkins wouldn't let me. I think I gets a good shot at his helmet though.

Tompkins is a good shit like that. He won't just leave you if you're drunk. I don't remember getting to the house at all. All I knows is the next morning I'm asleep in under the bedclothes with my jeans still on. I didn't get sick though, that's one good thing.

JENNIFER

I was a long time debating whether or not I should tell Mom about Chris staggering into the house last night. Steve had to practically carry him into the bedroom he was in such a state. But I guess I won't, not this time. There might just come a night when I'll want him to keep his mouth closed about something I've done.

For sure it wasn't because of his marks in school that he had any reason to celebrate. I knew he was going to fail, I could see it coming. Just what did he expect for the way he fooled around. I used to see him in the corridors between classes and he was forever making a nuisance of himself. He couldn't take a drink at the water fountain but he thought he had to put on a comedy act of some kind. Mom was foolish enough then to believe him when he said that he did most of his homework in school and that the twenty minutes he spent in his room at night was enough to get him by. Sure half the time he was gone out somewhere anyway.

I get pretty good marks, but they don't come without study. And studying is one thing I have to do as much of as I can this weekend. The rest of the students are out of school, but since this is the last year of high school for us, our class has provincial exams to write. I hate studying for them, but these exams might determine what first-year courses I'll have to do at university. I want to go in with as good a set of marks as I can get.

By Wednesday they'll all be over, thank God, and then I start work. I was jumping around for half an hour I was so happy after I found out that I got a job. It's not the best job in the world, but considering the fact that no more than half of the people in my class were able to come up with anything for the summer, I'm really happy about it. I should be able to save almost all the money I make.

This must be my lucky week. First on Tuesday I found out about getting the job, then on Wednesday night, around nine o'clock, the fellow I went with to the graduation dance phoned me up and invited me to go out with him this weekend. The truth is I only went with him to the graduation because it seemed like a really convenient situation for the both of us. I guess I was still thinking a lot about Scott at the time. Daryl was graduating too and each of us needed a date, so it ended up that we decided to go together. I'd known him for so long that I'd never even given much thought to going out with him, but it turned out we had a really great time. We went to the party after the dance was over and I didn't get home till four o'clock in the morning. Daryl's a bit shy, but he's a really nice fellow.

Last night he came over to the house around ten and we went out for a walk. It was a good break from studying. We were back again by eleven, but saying goodnight stretched out for a long time. Daryl does consider a girl's feelings, though, which is a switch from what a lot of fellows are like. He's not all hands just because he's alone with me. He makes me feel we can reason things out as we get to know each other. I know now I like him a lot.

What broke us up was the arrival on the scene of Chris and Steve. Daryl had to help Steve get him out of his coat and shirt. They took off his shoes and socks and just rolled him in under the covers. Steve looked a bit disgusted about having to lug him around like that, although he tried to convince me it wasn't all Chris's fault that he got as drunk as he did. I'd like to believe that. Mom is not far off the mark when she says Chris is a lot like his father.

9

CHRIS

Tompkins has been a good friend over the years. It's not everybody who would go out of their way like he did that Friday night to see that I got home. I knows that and that's why I don't feel the best about what's happened since then.

We had this argument and we quit hanging around together. See the worse thing about Tompkins is he always got to be home so early. And now that he's started work he's got even worse. Every night he wants to be home by eleven o'clock for frig's sake. He's got to get up by seven and if he stays out late then he's too tired the next day he says. That's no fun. I could be out till one and later and the old lady wouldn't care. As long as I shows up and she hears me come in. She'll call out from her bedroom, "Is that you Chris?" When I answers she'll tell me to lock the door and then she'll go back to sleep. Surprising how normal your voice can sound once you set your mind to it. Quite a few times lately the walk from the door to my bedroom hasn't been quite the steadiest.

I guess perhaps I had a few beer in me when the argument started. I wanted Tompkins to go halves on another six-pack and he said he wouldn't.

"Why not?" I asked him.

"Because I got to get some sleep if I'm going to be up on time. Last night it was twelve o'clock before I made it into the house and I was half dead all day at work."

"Com'on, you're gettin soft."

"It's okay for you, you can sleep in tomorrow."

"Scared of what your old man might say?"

"Slade, will you frig off. I'm goin. You comin or not?"

"Go on, I don't care what ya do. Make sure you kiss your mommy goodnight."

He stuck up his finger at me as he turned around and walked away. And he wasn't just fooling around like we do for a laugh sometimes.

"Suck me!"

He walked on home by himself. I just let him go on. I can't be going home at 11 o'clock for frig's sake.

But like I said—after, when I thought about it, I didn't feel the best about the way it happened. Maybe it was the beer.

But, I tell you what I've been doing the last few weeks. Stan Sheppard, he's had his licence for a good while so I guess he's about nineteen. Anyway, I've been hanging around a good bit with him and a couple of others. It started the night after the argument with Tompkins. I got aboard with him and a bunch of other fellows just to go for a ride and now it's sorta got to be a regular thing. The truth is I haven't seen much of Tompkins the last few weeks.

Stan, see he's got a Monte Carlo, a 305 automatic. She's second-hand, but she's a pretty decent machine. I should say *was* because now Stan's got the engine tore right to shit. She can still lay a good strip but she's not going to last him all that much longer the way he laces her. He's a friggin laugh though b'y. He had her doing 110 with eight of us aboard that first night coming down over Pinsent's Grade. It was one o'clock in the morning so there was not much chance of there being any cops around. Three weeks before and he could a buried the hand he said. I wouldn't doubt that one bit. Jesus, he don't slack. He does 80 sometimes going through Marten. I keeps telling him he's going to blow his motor again. But he don't give a shit. He's drawing his unemployment, and anyway his old man'll give him enough money to get another motor to put in her. That's the second one he's had in her now and he only bought the car five months ago.

It's a great laugh. I was getting sick and tired of walking or hitchhiking all over the place. Each of us chucks in a few bucks for gas and we're all set. I bet you last night we must a put close to 200 miles on the car. Four of us took off for Blakeside. That's about 40 miles away. You comes across some of the sleaziest-looking broads you'll ever lay eyes on walking the roads over there. You needs a combination lock on your zipper almost. We stopped and picked up a couple of them Stan knew from before and you talk about the hard-looking scouts. You'd be scraping for six months, I daresay, to get their eyeshadow off. But Stan don't give a shit what they looks like. They're all the same with a paper bag over their head he says.

I got to tell the truth though. I never done it with either one of them, not yet. I've been thinking about it. If I had a truck tire innertube for a safe maybe I would, because with them broads you never know what they got. Anyway, I'd rather do it with somebody I likes. Stan and Ed, they'd put the makes on a cow moose if they was drunk enough.

Last night when I got home it was close to 2:30. I wasn't drunk though. When Mom called out she sorta got half dirty cause it was so late. But she was too sleepy to put much life into it. I told her I was with Terry and he broke down for gas and we had to walk five miles. She believed me.

The only time I sees Mom much now is at dinner. It's 12 o'clock most days before I'm up outa bed. Usually it's just the two of us for dinner, cause if Jennifer is working day shift like she does mostly then she stays into the gas station and eats in the restaurant. Sometimes what we have for dinner Mom cooks herself, more times it's just out of a can. I wouldn't care so much if she'd only find chance to bake some bread now and then. And we never have any pies or anything like we used to before she went to work.

Before it seemed me and Mom always had a fair bit we could talk about. Now, I don't know what it is, but half she does is gab on and on about her job and complain about how tired she is. I'll help her out a bit around the house, like vacuuming the living room or something if I haven't got anything much to do. Then she's more likely to give me a bit of extra money. She complains sometimes but I usually gets it —three or four bucks a night. Sure if you buy a half dozen beer that's all of it gone right there.

Now and then she brings up about the old man. I thinks about him too sometimes. From what she says, he's making good money at the construction work he's doing and he gets lots of overtime. He must find it all right or he would a been back by now. I haven't been talking to him yet because I haven't been home anytime he's called. I just hope he don't get it in his head that he wants us all to move to the mainland.

It's pretty dull around the house these days compared to what it was before. I don't see Jennifer enough to get into a good racket with her anymore, now that she's working. You might say everybody is looking out to their own selves. That's all right with me just so long as the old lady don't start to get on my back about staying out late. I don't want to have to listen to that.

After the other day anyway I don't give much of a shit what she says to me. See the 25th of July came and went and nobody said a thing about it. I figured Mom was holding off till later on. I even came home a bit early that night expecting something. But she forgot about it. She never remembered it was my birthday. I turned sixteen for frig's sake and nobody even thought about it till the next day when I brought it up. The old lady said she remembered a few days before but she was so busy it slipped her mind. Slipped her mind. Not even a cake. Not that I'm tore up about cake but it's nice to get remembered like that. She gave me ten bucks when I told her about it the next day and she bought one of them frozen jobs and stuck a few candles on it.

I'm not fussy either about getting money for my birthday, although I did put it to good use —I got Stan to buy me a 26-ouncer of whisky out of it. I kept it till now so that we could take it with us on the trip tonight. See last week Stan got the idea of taking off into St. John's to see a rock concert in the stadium. Fish — they're a friggin good band and I wanted to see them really bad, only I knew the old lady wouldn't exactly grab the idea of me going with Stan. See she don't know yet I've been hanging around with him. I wouldn't a told her anything about it only Stan figured we'd take a tent and then camp overnight in some park some-where. He wants to make it a good tear while we're at it.

I never asked her about it really. What I done was leave a note on the table for her to find when she got off work. I told her I'd be back sometime tomorrow night. Once I was gone she couldn't do anything about it anyway. I don't care if she do get mad with me when I gets back.

It's a friggin good concert. This shitty band

come on first and made noise for a while, but Fish
are fuckin excellent. Fish is the best band this
Island ever put out. There's five of them and they
dress up like fishermen, only their oilskin outfits
must a cost a mint because they're all done over
with this glittery material that reflects the light all
over the place and they wear these silver-colour
rubber boots. It's enough to freak you right out.
And they've got the stage done up like a real fishing
wharf — barrels, nets, lobster traps, even a splitting
table with codfish on it. It almost *smells* like a friggin wharf. And for a backdrop then they got these
big screens with the sea painted on them, only the
way the light works it seems like the water is really
moving. Even the drums have lats all around them
like lobster traps and the outside of the organ is
made over to look like a ram's horn, what's used to
keep live lobsters in. It's a friggin wild idea.

I got right off on the way they started their
show. First, all you heard was the sea, and then
real quiet and slow they started playing this old
Newfoundland folksong, "We'll Rant and We'll
Roar," only they got it going faster and faster until
the lead guitar ripped into it and tore it right to
shit so that it came out sounding like it could
blow your fuckin head off. The light show is fantastic and halfway through the lead singer starts
firing out dried caplin into the audience, just like
some bands throw out scarves or hats or the way
the guy in Cheap Trick fires away guitar picks.
Talk about a laugh.

And the music is perfect. Music always

sounds ten times better anyway when you're stoned. Before we showed up to the concert we parked the car and spliffed some hash. Stoned is not the word. We're wrecked right out of our skulls. When we got inside we worked our way up front, practically on the stage. Jesus, it's a wild time — everybody right out of it, clapping their hands over their heads and jumping around. Enough tits flopping up and down that you'd need about ten sets of eyes to keep track of them.

The concert gets over about eleven. I could stay there another two hours easy. The band plays two songs when they come back the second time, but that's it. The yelling don't do no good and all the lights in the stadium comes on the one time, enough to burn out your friggin eyeballs. God, that's bad when you're stoned. You can't friggin come down that easy.

Lucky thing the campground isn't very far away. Stan and the others are so out of it I have to drive the car for them. I'm in no perfect shape myself but I'm better than what they are. I'm sure we go around in circles about ten times before we get on the main road to the highway. I didn't have a clue where we was going. I only was ever in St. John's twice before in my life. If I wasn't stoned I probably would a been scared of being stopped by the cops, but you know how it is — that hardly comes in your mind.

Trying to get the tent set up is another story. The tent is only the simple kind with the poles that go up on the outside. You couldn't have it any easier, but I bet a damn we're an hour getting it straight. None of the stupid poles seems to fit into one another right. And trying to find rocks then to beat down the pegs. And banging our friggin hands about ten times. And laughing then. We have the biggest kind of laugh over everything.

It's while we're laughing that the park warden comes down and tries to kick us out.

"You fellows—are you here to camp or create a racket?"

We don't see him until he's down the path and standing right up alongside of us with a flashlight in his hand.

"We paid to get in here just as well as anybody."

"That doesn't give you the right to keep other people from sleeping. Do you realize it's after twelve o'clock?"

"We don't give a shit. We're havin problems gettin the fuckin tent up," Stan says and we all busts out laughing.

"If you can't do it quietly then you'll have to leave."

"Who's going to kick us out — you?" And somebody laughs again.

"No, the RCMP. And if you fellows don't wise up with the language and cut out your brazenness, I'll be on that truck radio in two seconds and have them here."

That shuts things up a bit. He knows we can't afford to tangle with the cops.

When we don't say anything, only try again to

put up the tent and this time with not so much noise, he makes a move to leave. Not without a few more words though. "That's the only warning I'm giving you. If I come back again it'll be with the police."

The only thing we says to him is under our breaths. He goes off up the path. If he turned around he would see five juicy fingers stuck up at him. The jerk-face. Like Stan says, give them a uniform and a badge and you wouldn't know but they owned the goddamn world.

We get the tent up and the sleeping bags into it. We still have a dozen beer and a half bottle of whisky to get rid of yet. And I gets sick again. About three o'clock in the morning I have to go outside and it's raining. I don't have anything on, only a pair of shorts. And I'm throwing up for about ten minutes. Christ, do I ever get sick. It's the worst time my guts ever was. They're so friggin sore from throwing up. Half the reason is that stupid greasy chicken we had for supper.

I have to go back inside then wet, and get into the sleeping bag. I'm shivering half the friggin night. I'm up eight o'clock and dressed and in the car with the heater on trying to get warm. I'm not what you'd call sorry when they haul down the tent and stick it into the trunk. They leave the sleeping bags and the whole friggin works inside except for the beer bottles. They fire them in the woods. Good enough. I wouldn't be able to stand the sight of another beer bottle this early in the friggin morning.

10

MOTHER

One o'clock in the night and Chris is still not turned up yet from St. John's. He's got me worried half off my head. He's going to get one hell of a talking-to for taking off like that and not asking me if he could go. With Stan Sheppard no less. If there's one nuisance around this place it's that Stan Sheppard. No way am I going to have Chris hanging around with the likes of that.

It's got me so uneasy I had to call Frank and tell him I couldn't make it in to work. I suppose Frank got on all right tonight by himself. Perhaps he got one of the youngsters to give him a hand.

I haven't been able to do a tap of housework, nothing. All I've been doing is sitting here in the kitchen worrying about where he might be to. I tries to lie down, but I'm that tormented I got to get up again. I called Dorothy Tompkins earlier on because I thought Steven might a seen him, and when he said no, he didn't know where he was, that got me all the more uneasy. I can't sit still long enough to drink a cup of tea, that's how bad I am. And Jennifer walking around is no help.

I tells her to go on to bed.

If he don't turn up soon I'm going to have to call the Mounties. He could a been in a accident and I wouldn't know anything at all about it. That Stan drives like a maniac for God's sake. How in the world did Chris ever get mixed up with him I'd like to know? Him and Steven used to buddy around together for so long I didn't know but that was still who he used to be with in the night-time. But the way Steven was talking he's hardly laid eyes on him in the past few weeks.

I think that's a car door I hears closing. I hope to God that's him.

I opens the kitchen door to the porch and, my God, it's just as well if someone had hauled off and smacked me across the face. I wouldn't feel one bit more hurted or ashamed. There is Chris — mud all up one side of his clothes and the side of his face, barely able to stand up because he's loaded drunk. I wouldn't be able to call him my son because the way he is there he's not what I knows for my son.

"My God, Chris, what's wrong? What have you got done to yourself?"

When I opened the door he sprung up all of a sudden to try to look normal, but no way is he normal. You can smell beer on him worse than if someone had soaked his clothes in it.

"Chris, is you all right?" It frightens me, that's the truth. It's not like seeing Gord come home drunk, or any man for that matter. To see someone belong to me sixteen years of age in the condition he's in, I can tell you is more than enough to scare me. I calls out to Jennifer and then I takes hold of his arm to try and get him in the kitchen.

"Chris, answer me, is you all right?" I tries to keep him from falling down.

"Yes, I'm all right." As good as he can say it. His eyes is so glassy I have to make him look at me straight in the face to see there's not more the matter with them.

He won't sit down in the kitchen. He wants to go right into the bedroom. I tries to stop him before he gets to the hall. I'm not about to let him get away without some explanation.

"Let go. I'm goin to bed."

"Not before you tells me where you been."

"I'm goin to bed."

"Chris, sit down in that chair."

"Let go!"

He won't sit down, no way. And there's hardly anything I can do because he's strong enough now that I can't handle him anymore. He drags himself away from me and stumbles sideways against the wall. He almost lands on the floor. Jennifer tries to help him up but he pushes her out of the way.

"Where did you get the beer?" I shouts at him. If he's not going to try to be reasonable about it then he's going to have to listen to an earful from me. I follows him into the bedroom. "From that Stan Sheppard, wasn't it?"

"No."

"Tell me another lie now!"

"It wasn't Stan!"

"Then who was it?"

He collapses on the bed. "I found it," he mumbles.

"You found it! Chris, you can't expect me to believe that. You didn't just find it. Now who bought it for you?"

"I found the beer, goddamn it!" he yells.

"Stop your swearin at me!"

"I'm not fuckin swearin. I found the beer. Now leave me alone."

I feels like crying.

I couldn't get any more words out now if I tried. He don't have sense enough to be thinking right. He's not moving and his eyes are closed. I shakes him but he only moans.

He could pass out and die right there on the spot and I wouldn't know the difference. The only thing I can do is get him out of his clothes and into the bed. Jennifer helps me because he's too much for me to lift by myself. I never thought I'd have to do that, the same as if he was an infant, not able to do a thing for himself. I never felt so bad about anything in my life.

I don't close my eyes once for the night. All I got on my mind is Chris and the state he's in. I goes out to his bedroom three or four times during the night to see if he's still all right. The way he is perhaps he could smother himself, I don't know.

I don't understand it. You spends your life raising them the best way you knows how and then they're right ready to make a fool of everything you ever done for them. What I can't understand is how you can raise two children and them to turn out to be so different.

I can hardly believe it, to tell the truth, that he's got like he is. It's enough to break your heart. I knows he must have a few beer now and then. What teenagers don't growing up today. But to come home in the state he's in, my God, you can't help feel anything but ashamed. They haven't got sense enough now to know what they're doing to theirselves. He could have just as well spent the night in a ditch somewhere.

You knows he's going to hear something from me tomorrow. Until he gets old enough and gets out on his own he's not going to do just like he pleases, I'm telling him that. Perhaps that's half the reason he failed his grade ten. Sure I don't know. This drinking could a been going on for months and me not know anything at all about it. When he goes out of the house I don't know where he goes. Or how he spends his money, that's another thing. You got to trust them a certain amount. You can't pen them in.

CHRIS

When I come to life in the morning it was just the same as if my head was bolted onto the pillow and someone was hauling it tight with a wrench. I wanted to lie there like a dead dog for the rest of the day. I didn't want to bring all that misery up on two feet, but I knew I had to. My throat was dry and I was coughing and sneezing all at the same time. Plus my bladder was just about ready to bust apart.

I sat myself up at the side of the bed and it suddenly come to me that there was a lot better reason for not getting up. Something about Mom and last night. It didn't exactly flash into my brain as clear as a TV picture, but I could remember that she was there when I got home. She was supposed to be still at work or in bed or something. I must a been so stupid I never checked for lights before I come in. All I knows is that running into her face to face wasn't anything I was counting on.

I drained off about five gallons as quiet as I could in the bathroom and then I looked at myself in the mirror. There was some scratches on my face like I'd fallen down on some gravel. I couldn't remember how the frig they got there. And there was a chip gone off the corner of one of my teeth.

If I could a got in and out of the bathroom without making any noise it mightn't a been so bad, but as I was making my way back the old lady called to me to get dressed and come on out in the kitchen. Her voice wasn't quite overflowing with sweetness. God, for all the trouble it got me into, I might just as well have stuck my dick out the bedroom window.

Old mother don't spare no time before she cuts across me with her wonderful little bits of wisdom.

"Now my son, you sit down because there's a few things I'm going to say to you and they're not something you're going to want to hear."

"How about some breakfast?"

"Is that all you can think about? Here you staggered into the house at one-thirty in the morning, hardly able to see outa your two eyes and you thinks there's nothing else for me to do only get you your breakfast. What have you got to say for yourself, you just tell me that? What reason are you going to come up with for showing up in the state you was in last night?"

"No reason."

"What do you mean *no reason?* Where did you get the beer?"

"I found it."

"Yes, and in somebody else's hands. Now who bought it for you?"

I suppose she got a point there, but I'm not going to squeal on anybody so it's no good for her to try and get it out of me.

"I'm not going to say."

"You don't have to because I knows who it was — Stan Sheppard. How long have you been prowlin around with the likes o' that? You should have better sense. He's been nothin but a bloody nuisance since the day he was born. Now, my son, you listen to me. I don't want any more of this. If you haven't got sense enough to behave yourself when you're out night-time then you won't be leavin the house, supposin I got to bar the door to keep you in. And I don't want to see you go near that crowd

95

you've been hangin around with again. And don't think you're going to come to me lookin for money if all you're going to do is waste it on beer."

"What's wrong with a few beer?"

"There's a lot wrong with a few beer when you're only sixteen years of age! Do you want to end up in jail with a record for the rest of your life? At the rate you're goin that's just what you'll have."

I'll let her talk I suppose, let her get it out of her system. It was a pretty stupid thing to do I know, getting caught like that. I'll have to be more careful so's it won't happen again. But that ain't going to stop me from having a few beer with the fellows if I feels like it. Probably if I stuck to dope she wouldn't be able to tell so easy. I don't see why the frig she thinks she got to get so worked up about it anyway. If it was something good I done I daresay I'd have to wait till next year this time before she'd say anything about it.

"Now I hope you got this straight. If your father was here I wouldn't doubt but it'd be a darn sight more than a few words you'd have to deal with."

"He wouldn't have the face to do much the way he drinks."

"What your father does is his own business."

"And what I does should be mine."

"Christopher, my son, I got a darn good mind to hit you across the mouth. How did you ever get to be so saucy? Do you know who it is you're talkin to? It's your mother."

I don't say anything.

MOTHER

I just don't know what it is. I just don't know. What chance have you got raising youngsters like you wants them to be these days? You tries to do what you can for them and they'll look at you and sauce you then just like you're someone they never seen before in their life.

I'm fed up with it, that's the god's truth. I knows where the attitude they got comes from certainly. The TV programs for one thing. You can't switch on the TV but there's someone swearing and arguing. And that's not half of what they hears out around. From what I can tell the movies that gets showed in that community hall are a shade worse. They're nothing better than skin flicks half of them.

There was a time when this place could a been called quiet. You'd only ever see a Mountie perhaps once a week. But now, there's not a night goes by but there's a police car going back and forth the road. It's getting so now that you soon won't be able to walk the streets. And there's another thing. That campground over in Spencer's Harbour. Every weekend in the summer that place is blocked with troublemakers from one place and another. More dope and beer floating around. You'd think the town council'd have better sense than to let them in.

Perhaps I should quit my job.

If Chris don't smarten up then I'll have to.

I'd quit right now except for Frank. I don't want to see him stuck with nobody. He keeps telling me I'm the most reliable person he's ever had working for him.

Except for Frank. I guess that's just it — except for Frank. I likes Frank. Frank is the first man that's treated me like that since I can't remember when. I knows I shouldn't even be thinking about it. But it's there and I've got to face it. Since his wife died he's been lonely. I could tell that the day he offered me the job. If I had any sense I would a turned it down then and there and there'd be none of this to even think about. We've spent hours some afternoons when I goes in early just talking — about his wife dying and how the children took it and other things. It's not easy for a man to raise a family on his own. He's got three still going to school and he's got to try and keep house and make a living for them too. It's hard, I knows it must be.

But how can I get involved with Frank. All I got to do is make one move and he would, I'm sure he would. Gord is gone I knows, but my God, he's my husband and I've got two children to think about. What in the world would they think if they ever found out?

11

JENNIFER

According to the radio the exam results were released yesterday, and if the post office can do its job for once they should be here this morning. The mail is sorted by 10:30 so I was dressed and out of the house by twenty after.

Chris was just dragging himself out of his bedroom when I left. I've seen people hung over before but that was disgusting. I hope Mom gave him a good lecture. I haven't seen her that mad in a long time. He needs to be tamed down a bit and she knows it.

As I come in sight of the post office I seem to be getting worse with every step. I shouldn't be so nervous because I know I passed. That isn't the question. What's worrying me is how high my marks are going to be. I know I didn't write a very good French exam, the oral part fooled me up, and that could be something to bring my average down. Once I'm inside the post office I don't waste any time in opening the box, and sure enough it's there. Who would think one thin envelope could mean so much to anyone? Once I have it in my hands I close the box and come right out of the post office again. I have to be out of sight of everybody.

A few minutes later I run in the house, so excited I could scream.

"I passed, I passed — 89.5 average!" I yell as I come running through the kitchen door.

It's like bursting through the door of a morgue. But Mom brightens up right away. "Oh my heavens, that's not right, is it?"

"Yes, look — 92, 94, 80, 87, 96, and 88."

"Jennifer, that's wonderful." She hugs and hugs me and kisses me again. "I'm some proud of you, my dear, I'm some proud!"

"Oh God, I'm so excited. Eighty-nine and a half percent, I can't believe it."

Chris is sitting at the table brooding over a glass of orange juice. Mom must have dished him out quite the sermon because he doesn't bother to so much as look at me. He pushes back his chair and gets up to go to his bedroom again.

"Well, aren't you even going to congratulate your sister?" Mom says. "Or is that too much to expect?"

He doesn't answer her. Let him go on if he's that contrary. He's turned sulky now because the little dear got told off, I suppose. It's about time if you ask me.

"You think we'll ever see the day when you come into this house with marks like that?" Mom asks him. "Not likely."

Not likely is right. I tell her not to waste her

breath. But what I have to do right now is phone Daryl. We promised each other last night that the first thing either one of us would do when we found out our marks would be to phone up the other person.

CHRIS

Who the hell gives a shit what marks she got? Not me for sure. So she got brains, she goddamn well don't mind bragging about them, though, do she? That Jennifer turns my friggin guts. I'll be glad when she goes to university and out of my sight. I'd rather congratulate a friggin goat.

I went back in the bedroom, closed the door and locked it. I took off my clothes and crawled back in the bed again. I never had a head on me before like I had this time. I wish the hell everybody would just leave me alone.

And I'm not in bed a half-hour when the old lady comes banging at the door. What the hell do she want this time? She said enough to me already this morning to keep my eardrums ringing for a solid month.

"Chris, get out here right away."

"I'm trying to get some sleep. Leave me alone."

"There's someone at the door who wants you — a policeman."

First I don't think I could a heard it right. A cop, what do a friggin cop want with me? I just hope to God the old lady haven't called the cops to find out about the beer. I don't suppose she could be stun enough for that. What else could it be? I try to think back over the last few days. Last night after I got so drunk — things do get a little hazy there. But I'm pretty sure we wasn't at anything besides drinking. Stan never had no accident, not that I knows anything about.

I gets into my jeans and shirt and opens up the bedroom door. Mom is standing up right there.

"Now what's this all about?" she says, right ready to pitch into me again, without even giving me so much as a chance to button up my shirt.

That means she couldn't a been the reason he was there. "I dunno," I tell her.

"What do you mean you don't know? You didn't get into some kind of trouble and not tell me, now did ya?"

"No."

"I hope you're tellin me the truth."

"I told ya — I don't know why he wants to see me."

"Well go on and find out."

On top of all this so far, and now for a cop to have to show his face in the house. A cop is not exactly someone I'm willing to fool around with. I goes to the front door and pushes open the screen door with one arm. It's a Mountie all right — tall and with a moustache like they all have, but looking so serious you'd swear I'm up for murder or something.

"Are you Christopher Slade?" he asks me.

"Yes, sir."

"I'd like to talk to you for a few minutes."

"Yes, sir." I'm a bit scared, to tell the truth.

"In my car."

"Oh." I'm just going to step outside, when I remember I don't even have anything on my feet. "I better go get my sneakers or something." I goes back into the house as he walks towards the car.

"What do he want?" the old lady says, as soon as the door closes.

"He wants to talk to me in his car."

"What for?"

"He didn't say."

"Well, hurry up. Don't keep him waiting. And whatever he asks you, you tell him the truth. Don't you go tellin him any lies, do you hear me."

"Yes!" I got to say something to her to get her off my back. Frig, I wish she'd just keep quiet and let me handle this.

It's probably bad enough getting questioned by a cop knowing what he's going to be asking you, but I haven't got a sweet clue what he wants. I really don't.

When I gets to the car he's already inside behind the steering wheel with a clipboard in his hands. I opens the passenger door and sits across from him. I'm trying not to look nervous, but I am. I'm nervous as hell.

"Could you tell me what you want me for? I didn't do anything."

"I just want to ask you a few questions."

But first, before he does anything else, he

reads out what he says is a "police caution," telling me what my rights are. Christ, it's starting to sound more serious all the time. He writes down my full name and address and my age and my parents' names and phone number and all that. He takes his own dead time making sure every word is spelled exactly right. Will you get to the point I keep saying in my mind, get to the point.

Then he asks me, "Were you with a fellow by the name of Stanley Sheppard last night?"

"Yes." I knew it had to be something about him.

"For how long?"

"All night, till about 1:30, I guess."

"And what were you doing?"

"Just drivin around with him, in his car."

"Here in Marten?"

"We was in Blakeside and Spencer's for a while, and then we come back here."

"At what time?"

"I don't remember exactly."

"Before ten o'clock?"

"No, after, I think."

He's rhyming off question after question and here I am just sitting still, shooting out answers as fast as I can. I don't know for a minute what the hell he's driving at.

"Do you remember where you were at about 12 o'clock?"

"No."

"Why not?"

"I fell asleep in the car." That's the truth, I

did. I must have, I can't seem to remember anything anyway.

"Were you drinking last night?"

"No, sir." That's my first reaction. I knew he was going to be asking that. What else could I say? I don't want to be charged with drinking under age. Plus I might be getting somebody else in trouble if I says I was.

"Are you sure of that?"

"Yes, sir."

"There were empty beer bottles in the car."

Shit. Now I don't know what to say. Probably he's already been talking to Stan and the other fellows. And what did they tell him? If they told him something different and he figures out I'm lying then that's not going to look so good, now is it?

"I might have had a few beer . . . I thought you meant hard liquor." It's the only way I can think of to get out of it. I can just picture the old lady now if she could a heard that.

"Did you or didn't you?"

"Yes, I did."

"How many?"

"I don't remember."

"More than a half dozen?"

Shit, he don't give up, does he? "Maybe, I don't remember."

"Where did you get the beer?"

"They was in the car. I don't know where they come from."

It sounds pretty dumb I know, but how can he expect me to squeal on someone else. He don't press the point, thank God. But it's probably only because he knows the answer already.

"Is the beer what caused you to go to sleep?"

"I was tired too. I didn't get very much sleep the night before."

"Okay, we'll leave the beer part for now." He stops the questions for a moment and writes down something else. Then he says, "Tell me this — do you remember being in and around Blackmore High School at any time last night?"

That sorta throws me off. I don't know what he could be driving at. "No, sir."

"Do you know anything about any windows being broken out there?"

"No, sir." I don't, and that's honest.

"Well, there were a total of eight windows smashed out at the rear of the school last night and I have a report that Stan Sheppard's car was in there at about the time that it happened."

"I don't know anything about it. That's the truth."

"And I have another statement that says you were in the car at that same time."

Now what the frig is going on. Windows, I don't know anything about any windows. "I didn't break no windows, I can tell you that."

"Could it be that you were so drunk you didn't know what you were doing?"

"I was asleep in the car. You can ask any of the other fellows who was there."

"Are you sure?"

"I'd know if I done it even if I was drunk."

"Are you sure?"

"Yes. I think so."

"But are you certain?"

I don't know what the frig to say. "No" is what comes out.

"And were you drunk?"

"I don't remember."

"You know you might as well give me the truth. You've already made one statement that you've had to change. What I want is the truth. I'll tell you right now — if you're lying and it's proved you lied, then it's not going to look very good in court."

"In court?"

"Yes."

"But I didn't break no windows."

"Even if you didn't, you can still be charged with drinking under age."

That gets me shitbaked altogether. Court. Wait till the old lady hears this one.

He asks me a few more questions and I have to make a full statement about last night and sign it, but it all comes to the same thing. Someone smashed a pile of windows out of the high school and sprayed red paint all over one end of the building, and by the looks of things the boys in the car was the ones that done it. But what I told him to write down is true. I swear it is. I can't remember being there. I didn't break no windows, not that I knows anything at all about. I couldn't a been that far gone, for God's sake.

I knows one thing though — I'm into it up to

my neck now and that's for sure. This is the first time for me ever being in any trouble with the cops and it don't exactly feel very healthy. Christ, and to have to go to court too.

I'd sooner be slung over a wharf in a brin bag than have to tell the old lady that. But she's going to have to find out. If not from me then from someone else. Thank God the old man's not around.

But even so, the least she can do is try to be reasonable about it. Instead of that she just about takes the friggin head off me. It wasn't my fault, for frig's sake, she should be able to see that. But she won't listen. It's just as well if I never even said I was sorry.

"You mean to tell me you could a been one of the ones that was in on breakin out the windows and you don't know anything at all about it?"

"I don't think I would a done something like that as drunk as I was."

"You don't *think*. You don't *think*. How bad do it make me feel, how bad in the name of God? How ashamed do you think I am? Sometimes I thinks I'm more ashamed than you are, yes I do. And it's not like you don't know any better. You just don't care, that's all there is to it, you just don't care."

"Care about what?" What the frig is that supposed to mean?"

"Care about yourself for one thing. Where do you think you're going to end up if you keeps on going like this?"

"Who said it was going to happen anymore?"

"At the rate you're . . ."

I lets her go on and on. I just sits there in the kitchen trying to make it look like I'm listening to her. She goes on for so long that I can't put up with it anymore. I takes off in the bedroom and slams the door. For frig's sake, I knows what I done was stupid, if I done it. But a fellow can make a few friggin mistakes, can't he? Or do we all have to be perfect little darlings like Jennifer.

12

CHRIS

I knows it was pretty dumb, getting into trouble like this. What scares me is that I still can't get it straight in my head exactly what happened. I knows for sure I went to sleep in the car. I'm positive of that much. But about the only other thing I can remember is the empty beer bottles banging back and forth on the floor by the back seat. Whether or not I come to and done something else, I haven't got a clue. I don't think I did. But it don't exactly feel very smart having to tell people you don't know for sure what you was doing.

The next week has got to be one of the worse ones I ever punished through. The old lady started off by saying she didn't want me going out in the night-time. I thought it over a lot, but I went on anyway. Just how could she expect me to stick it in the house alone on a summer's night. I made it a point just the same of being home and in bed before she got off work, and I stayed clear of Stan except to talk to him through the window of his car. He was laughing off the whole thing, like getting caught at what they'd done was the greatest joke in the world. To tell the truth, to me it didn't seem so friggin funny. Stan got after me to go over to Blakeside again with them. I told them no.

Actually I didn't end up doing a hell of a lot when I went out in the nights. The story about what happened was out around town and I couldn't walk down the road but it looked to me like everybody was just ready to pounce on me with a pile of questions. I had to try and look a bit cool when they asked me about it, otherwise they'd get the idea I was scared shitless, and who wants that.

I felt like calling up Tompkins and having a talk with him. I needed someone who I could talk to. In fact I went to the phone two or three times and almost dialed his number, but I didn't because after a few weeks of pretty much ignoring him it didn't seem the best thing to be doing. I ran into him for a while one night but he was with a girl, Cathy Delaney, and some others. It looked to me like he'd found a new bunch to spend his time with.

I laid off the beer pretty well, that's one thing. All I drank was what someone else offered me and then it was only a few. I consider that was cutting back a good bit. I was nowheres near feeling anything either night and that's good for me. That should a been enough to get her off my back.

But no way. The old lady never did let me forget about having to go to court. And when the cop showed up with the summons later on in the week that was just what she needed to set her back on full throttle again. I tell you it was enough to send anybody up the wall. Good thing she was gone by four o'clock in the afternoon because I'd never a been able to put up with that all day. I would a run away, I'm not kidding.

Every morning that week she'd have a whole load of things lined up for me to do around the house. Work to keep me busy and out of trouble she said. She even got it in her head for me to paint the inside of the house, the kitchen no less, with all the cupboards and crooks and corners. It was a full two days' work and I worked at it then like a slave. If that would a been the end of it I wouldn't have minded. But even before the kitchen is dry she's got the green paint bought for my bedroom and the brush in my hand. I'll never see the last of it.

Even when I'm scotin my guts out she hardly seems satisfied. It's like she got something else on her mind half the time. And it's not just me having to go to court, I knows it's not. I don't know what it is, but just because she's pissed off about something else don't mean she got to take it all out on me.

What saves me is a call from Rev. Wheaton. He's the last person in the world I expected to have phone me. I feels funny talking to him first, guilty I suppose, because I haven't been to church in so long. He must a noticed that. And about having to go to court, I wouldn't doubt but he knows about that too. But he don't mention either one of it. What he wants to know is whether or not I'm still interested in going to camp as a counsellor. That's hardly crossed my mind since the beginning of the summer. I was all fired up about it for a long time after camp last year, but then after I quit being a server I figured that Rev. Wheaton had just dropped my name. You'd think he'd have second thoughts about asking me, especially considering the trouble I'd managed to find for myself to get into.

But he don't have to mention it to me a second time. Anything to get away from the house for a while. Camp is starting on Wednesday he says, and that's only four days away. That's all that keeps me going while I works my way through the gallons of paint.

On Sunday I decided I'd go to church — a little warm-up before camp. The eight o'clock service in the morning no less. It's the first time I've been to church in weeks. Actually it was all right too. I was up and out of the house and back again before anybody knew I even left. The communion service was quiet with no hymns, and, best of all, there wasn't many people there to look at you.

MOTHER

In another hour I'll have to get Chris on the move if he's going to camp. They told him to be ready by ten o'clock. I guess I done the right thing by phoning Rev. Wheaton. I had to have someone other than Frank to talk to about all this. Rev. Wheaton said that he thought Chris might want to go to the boy's camp with him, as a counsellor. I knew before that he had it in his mind to go, but he hadn't mentioned it in so long that I forgot all about it. Perhaps ten days up there'll do something to help straighten him out.

I knows I could certainly use ten days of not having to worry about him. That's a fact. I've almost had to give up speaking to him because he's got that contrary he don't want to hear one word from nobody. I'm doubtful if all I've been saying has been doing him any good. It's probably going in through one ear and out through the other. But I've got to keep after him because he's just liable to go and do something worse.

I've got him painting the inside of the house now. That keeps him busy for so long, but once I leaves the house for work then there's no way of me knowing where he goes. He's in bed asleep when I gets home, but I don't know but he's back at the beer again. See you can't tell him anything. He thinks he's too old now to be told. If he had a few grains of sense he wouldn't be in the trouble he's into now. There's Steven over there, the nicest kind of young fellow. I said to Chris, you don't see Steven running around all hours of the night getting into trouble. That got him mad, but I don't care. He's put me through enough misery these last couple of months that he darn well deserves all the lectures he gets from me.

Ten days should give me time to get straightened away. Frank's been after me to take a couple of days off and rest up, but this is still a busy time and it's just too much work for one person to handle right. If he can't keep up with the orders then it's not going to be good for business. He's invested in a new fryer now and things like that don't come cheap. I don't like not being there when I knows he needs me.

That's the trouble I guess, when you comes to size it all up — not being able to quit. Frank should know better than to think that this what's started between the two of us can go on for very much longer. Something's got to be done, one way or the other. Give it up altogether, either that or tell Gord it'd be better if we was separated. I can't live like I am now. Before long someone is going to find out and then it'll be too late. That would make a fine piece of gossip, now wouldn't it, the way some people talks around this place.

I've got myself to think about. I've got my family to think about. These seventeen years with Gord haven't been bad ones. We've got two children to show for it. Sometimes I wonder, though, if we'd ever a been married at all if it wasn't for me being pregnant with Jennifer. I don't know but I wouldn't a gone away somewhere to work and met somebody else. Of course it's no use thinking about that now. What's done is done. I have to put my mind on the present.

Gord's been gone now over three months. He said the last time he phoned he'll be back before long. He'll work double shifts so he can get some time off to fly home. He says if he can't find any work around here this time then we're all packing up and moving to Calgary. Now that's about the last thing in the world I wants to hear.

I haven't told Chris about that yet. Of course it don't make that much difference to Jennifer. She'll be gone to university in September anyway. She's already got her residence application and everything accepted.

When I told Gord about Chris having to go to court he just about went off the head. If he had any doubts at all in his mind about coming home, then, I daresay that got rid of them quick enough. He said Chris was the last person he thought would go and do something like that. Only thing is, like I told Gord, Chris is changed, and it's not for the better by any means. He phoned one morning just to have a talk to him. It was only six o'clock by their time. Here it was 9:30 and I had Chris up and out of bed so's he could get the painting in the kitchen finished. I don't know what Gord had to say to him but it wasn't too pleasant, you can be guaranteed that. Chris said about ten words and all the rest come from the other end. When he finally hung up the phone he wasn't very well pleased. He found out it wasn't only me he let down by what he done. It takes a lot for his father to get mad with him, but when he do he knows only too well that he means it.

PART TWO

13

CHRIS

When I got aboard the bus for camp I set my mind on leaving the whole darn works of my headaches home. Slam the door on everything that's been getting under my skin. First the old lady. And then Dad. I didn't expect the old man to go jumping down my throat so bad as he did. I wouldn't doubt one bit now Mom put him up to it. I wouldn't put it past her, that's for sure. He wouldn't even stop to listen to my side of the story. All he kept doing was butting in and saying how I should a had better sense. And swearing his head off. If he'd been sensible about it, I might a tried to explain a few things, but after a while I just give up on it.

If there's one thing I always liked about camp it's the fact that the minute you set foot there it's like being put in another world. A thousand and one things could be going on outside, but you don't know nothing about it. It's just as good as a ten-foot fence. And by this time eighty miles and a ten-foot fence between me and home is just what I wants.

The Marten intersection was the fourth stop the bus made and already it was about three-quarters full with kids. I walked down between the seats with my knapsack and sleeping bag and piled them in the back with the rest. Mainly I was on the lookout for anyone I'd seen at camp before. None of the campers I knew because they were all too young, but I thought maybe there'd be somebody else on the staff who'd been there as a camper some year when I was. One fellow's face I recognized — Dwight Strickland. I remembered him from camp two years ago.

"Strickland, how's it goin?" I says, and slides into an empty seat in front of him. He's sitting sideways across two seats, smoking, with the smoke drifting out through the open window behind him. Actually he's one of the last people I would ever have expected to find coming back to camp. "Whata you doin here? Counsellor?"

"Yeah. You?" I nod. "That's decent."

He never struck me to be the type that got off on camp enough to want to work as a counsellor. All I ever remember him doing was sneaking smokes and complaining about the food.

"Think there'll be any broads at this camp?" he says. "That's half the reason I came. That and being bored with nothing to do all summer."

Some years a female or two show up to add a bit of spice to the surroundings. "Perhaps that swimming instructor who was here two years ago will be back," I tell him.

"You mean Flipper. I never did find out her

real name. Yeah, she was a decent piece of gear. With my luck this year we'll end up with a 250-ton blimp of some kind. Someone they'll have to name The Titanic or something."

I laugh. "How many campers, do you know?"

"Eighty-five or ninety I heard that guy say. Listen," he adds, "they don't expect us to put up with too much shit from them, do they?"

I grin. "You mean, like being drowned in Pepsi?"

"Yeah, crap like that." He's serious. He really is.

From what I remember that was a pretty good laugh. That was the year Strickland was at camp. I got the fellows in our cabin together one canteen break and we decided we'd have a little fun with Slink, one of the counsellors. He was a pretty decent guy, but you know, anything for a bit of fun. We each had a can of Pepsi hid under the bunks when he showed up for his regular after-noon bull session. He laid back in one of the bunks, and after giving him a few minutes to talk his way through a couple of Eatmores, up we got and grabbed into him and dragged him out to the middle of the floor. He was no small size, way bigger than either one of us, but what could he do against eight fellows. We each took turns then with a can of Pepsi — shook it up good, banged it on the floor a couple of dozen times and then took aim on him. Drowned the poor bugger like I said. All over his clothes, his head, up his nose some of it, and the last can right down inside his shorts. I must say he took it pretty good for someone with their balls floating in Pepsi. We opened the door and let him up after that. Off he goes across the field, one of the boys yelling out, "Slink had a wet dream!" at the top of his lungs.

Rev. Wheaton marched across the field fifteen minutes later when he heard about it, ready to bawl us out, but by that time we had the cabin mopped up and looking like it never even seen the sight of a drink can. He never said much. As long as nobody got hurt or nobody left a mess he didn't freak out too much. It was a different story now the time cabin five beat a hole through the door with a broom handle. Talk about see sparks fly.

The bus arrives at the campsite at about 1:30. After a couple of minutes Rev. Wheaton comes over. "Chris . . . and Dwight is it . . . you made it on the bus okay? Good. You fellows want to get settled away in the staff hut. Pick a room and put your gear in there. And if you see any campers around, tell them they should all be in the main building for registration."

In the staff hut we meet the other three fellows who will make up the junior staff. I remember one of them but the others are new to me. All of them seem like pretty decent guys though. They already have their rooms picked out and Strickland takes it as a natural thing that me and him should share the same room. I don't say no, that would seem a pretty snotty thing to be doing, so I just follow him inside and toss my gear on the floor.

The first thing he does is lie back on the bottom bunk and have a smoke. The guy is a regular tilt. Between draws he digs through an overnight bag and hauls out an 8-track player and about twenty different tapes. He picks out one tape, April Wine, and jams it in the 8-track. I like April Wine, I mean he got it a bit loud even for me, but I figure just starting camp and everything there's a lot more interesting things to be doing than just lying around smoking and listening to music.

I do a toss off the top bunk and head off out to check and see what the others are up to. They're just going out the door, down to where the senior staff is registering the boys. Me and the other fellow who's been here before, Craig, gives the other two the lowdown on what each of the buildings are — the crafts hut, the chapel, the dining hall, the path down through the woods to the swimming area and the other one which takes you to a small wharf and the shed where the canoes are stored.

Of course you get all kinds of boys showing up at camp. Some are shy and don't talk much, some others have been here before and are chasing each other around like someone just let them off their leashes. Some, you can tell, are going to be tough nuts for the whole camp, just by the way they stand around working at being pests already.

One kid comes up to me and says, "You a counsellor, buddy?"

"Yeah."

"How would you like to get massacred the first night by a few of us campers." He jumps around with his fists up, faking a few boxing moves.

A real winner of a kid. "How about we put this guy on dishes . . . permanently."

That don't scare him off either. He still swings his fists around like he's itching to take a smack at me.

"Go over there look, and see can't you find a tree to tie yourself to." It's going to be a fun week, I can see that.

After a while Rev. Wheaton shows up to talk to us. "Everything okay?" he says. "Looks like you'll have plenty to keep you busy. When you get chance now boys, go around, talk to the campers, get to know them, especially the ones who haven't been here before. Some of them are still a bit scared, the first time away from home and not sure what to expect, you know what it's like. Okay?" Then he looks just at me. "Chris, I'd like to talk to you for a moment if I could. Could you come over here?"

He starts walking across the field. I strolls along next to him. I knew this was going to come sooner or later.

"I haven't seen much of you in the last couple of months. How have you been?"

"Okay, I guess."

We walk for a while before he stops and says, "Don't want to talk about it?"

"Not much to talk about."

"Okay. That's fine. Perhaps later on we can have a chat?"

I shrugs my shoulders. He don't press the point. One thing about him — he knows when not to start bugging people.

"Chris, how many years is this now you've been coming to camp?"

"This is my fourth year."

"What were you — thirteen when you came first?"

"Yeah, something like that."

"Were you ever homesick?"

"Not much. A little the first day. After that I was okay."

"That's good. Well, most of these boys here are eleven and twelve. That's a bit younger. What I have is a small job for you, and I think with three years' experience as a camper you're probably a good one for it."

He turns around, facing the campers. "There's a young boy here, his name is David Morrison. He's over there, see him, with the glasses, sitting on his duffle bag? He's barely eleven and he's come to camp by himself. What does he look like to you?"

"Homesick."

"That's about right. He's already come up twice to me and said, 'Sir, I wants to go back . . . sir, can I call somebody to come and get me?'"

"Shouldn't let him do that."

"No, you're right. We don't want to give in to him, not at this point. He's got to give himself a chance. Now, what I would like for you to do is have a talk with him, see what you can do to help him get over this problem. That might be all he needs — a friend, someone he can talk to."

"Yeah, that could be."

"Will you try it?"

"Okay . . . yeah, I spose I can give it a shot."

"Good."

And before I knows anything Rev. Wheaton is gone off somewhere else, leaving me with this little job all in my own hands. I'm not used to trying to get buddy-buddy with an eleven-year-old kid, especially one that I never seen before. When I looks at him he don't seem in much of a mood for an instant cure.

"Hey David, whata ya doin?"

He looks up at me and then the head sinks down again. "How did you know my name?" he says.

"I dunno, somebody told me. Not feeling too happy, are ya?"

He won't answer. I'm getting the feeling he's not exactly big on conversation.

"What's wrong, something got your tongue?"

"Nothing's wrong!"

"Malaria?"

"There's nothing the matter, so you can go on."

What are you supposed to say to someone as thickheaded as that?

"Where you from?"

He mumbles something.

I try to repeat it. "That's a strange name."

"Carbonear," he says, almost yelling. "Carbonear. You deaf or what?"

"Take it easy with the vocal cords, old man. Nice place?"

"It's okay."

"Any half-decent looking girls there?"

I gets half a smile with that one.

"Well, are there? Com'on, I might be over there sometime."

"A few."

"Nice asses on them or what?"

He actually laughs. Now how was that for strategy.

"Listen, wanta hear a good joke? . . . Well, do you?" I have to talk fast, now that I've started something.

"I don't care." He don't say it with much life, but at least he's talking.

I tell him a short little dirty one of some kind. Nothing really so dirty that his young mind can't handle it. It gets a bit of a laugh from him.

"Have you registered yet?"

"I'm not going to register."

"Why not?"

"I don't know if I'm staying."

"Sure, you're staying. You'll like it here once you gets to know a few people. Once you're assigned to a cabin you'll have a whole crowd of new friends."

That don't impress him much. I sees it's going to take something more than that. "Do you like canoeing?" I ask him.

"I've never even been canoeing."

"How about after supper we go out on the river for a while?"

"I don't know anything about it."

"I'll teach you."

That does something to stir up his brain, finally.

"Okay?"

"Okay . . . I guess."

He gets at the end of the registration line a while after that. Still not very lively, but at least it's a start. I guess I done some good.

About an hour later I dodge off over to number three cabin. That's where he's ended up, with six other boys. He's the odd fellow out, though — the others came in pairs, each with a friend they knew before. That's okay. Give him time and he'll fit in. Just takes a while to get to know each other.

When I comes in he's on a bottom bunk, with his gear next to him, none of it unpacked. The others have at least their sleeping bags spread out across the bunks. And he's the only one not getting ready for the general swim that's going ahead before supper.

"Hey Morrison, goin for a swim or what?"

"Can't swim."

"Any good at gettin wet?" Some of the others laugh, but not him.

"Com'on, we're all goin," one of them says.

"I don't have to go if I don't want to!"

I lets the swimming bit drop. Can't get on his back. I could look at it another way, I suppose — at least he's not crying.

"Well boys, time for the survey."

"What survey?"

"What survey? Did somebody say what survey? For supper, of course. Now, how many want their steaks well done?"

"We're having steaks for supper! "Some of their eyes pop open.

"Yeah, didn't you hear the announcement? Now, how many want theirs well done?"

"He's bullshitting."

"I am not. Now, com'on, I have to report back to the kitchen. You can have it either well done, medium, or rare. Now how many for well done?"

That gets one sucker to put up his hand. "One . . . that all? How many for medium?"

"I wants mine well done."

Now we're getting somewhere. "That's two for well done. Three now. I'd wish you'd make up your minds. Four . . . boys I'll never get this straight. And you others — medium or rare? Medium. Medium. What about you Morrison?"

"I'm not goin to get sucked in," he says, still pretty quiet.

I stare at him but manage to keep a straight face. "Morrison, now I ask you, do I look like someone who'd try to suck anybody in?"

"Yes."

"Do you want a steak or don't you?"

"There's no steaks. Boys, it's only bull what he's saying."

"How much do you want to bet?"

"I'll bet you a canteen," he says, stirred up all of a sudden. "If there's no steak you'll have to pay for my canteen tomorrow."

How am I going to get out of this one? The little turkey figures he's got me cornered. "I'm not allowed to bet. It's against camp rules. No counsellor is allowed to make bets with a camper."

"Lies."

"Okay, we'll see. . . . That's four well done and two medium and I wants mine rare. Morrison don't get any."

"What's your name anyway?" he asks me.

"Chris."

"Chris, you're full of bull."

"I'll remember that. Insulting a counsellor. Automatic two days on dishes. Boys, the rest of you are okay. Morrison is the one in trouble." I should be careful not to press my luck with this. I have the others sucked in good with the steaks, now they're starting to get suspicious again.

The PA buzzes on then announcing lineup for a general swim. Saved by the bell. The other six are out the door, all making vicious threats about what they'll do if no steaks show up on their supper table.

"Com'on, let's go," I tell Morrison.

"You're fakin, I knows you're fakin."

He don't tire easy, that's one thing I can say for him.

"You know what I do to people like you?"

"What?"

"I make mincemeat out of their brains."

132

"If I tried it on you I wouldn't have a job," he laughs, the first real laugh I've seen from him.

"Ah, a little smart ass." I nails him with a few smacks as we're going through the door. "And the kid likes pressing his luck."

"The kid don't get sucked in."

"We'll see about that." He chases me halfway across the field before I gets so far ahead that he can't catch up. He seems to be coming along. Give him a full day and he should be okay.

14

CHRIS `

At the supper table the young fellows in cabin three are threatening to slaughter me as soon as dessert is finished. All except Morrison who's happy enough with the glory of being the only one I hadn't suckered in.

Supper is goulash. It's really steak I try to tell them, ground up and mixed with just a few other ingredients. That's followed by the usual highlight of the first mealtime at camp — the naming of the staff. Each of us gets the privilege of being christened with a camp nickname, to be used by the campers for the whole time we'll be together. From the years I can remember the same ones kept turning up, names like Flipper or Jaws for the person who does the swimming, and Mr. Chips or Woody or something for the guy who works at crafts. Rev. Wheaton asks for suggestions. They flood in from all parts of the dining hall. He clamps down on this shouting match and then they take a vote on two or three. For me, since I'm pretty average in height and weight, my hair is not blond, and I don't have any outstanding

physical features like a 10-inch nose, it's got to
have something to do with canoeing. That's what
he tells them I'll be working at. You'd think things
would stay logical like that. But one guy from
cabin three shouts out "Meatballs," another
"Meathead." Then finally "Beefbrains." And that's
what they decide on — Beefbrains. The guys at
the table all laugh like it's the best joke they've
heard all day. They figure they've paid me back.

After supper, that's all I can hear as I'm leaving the dining hall — Beefbrains repeated over and
over by every kid who comes near me. Morrison is
the one who gets the biggest charge out of it
because he claims he's the one who came up with
the name in the first place. For the fun he seems
to be getting from it, I figure I'll let him bug me
longer than the standard fifteen seconds before
threatening to give him a rough face lift. Even
though he's the most stubborn person I've ever
run across, one thing I likes about the kid is that
he's a bit on the ball with the jokes. Not much of
the stuff you'd expect from a kid that age.

I takes him out canoeing after supper. I have
to do it a bit on the sly because otherwise I'd
have a dozen campers down my neck complaining
that they're not getting a fair deal. We take out a
15-foot fiberglass and first I have to show him the
right way to get in and lay down a few laws about
keeping his weight in the centre and not moving
around like it's an oil tanker or something
he's aboard. I must say, though, he catches on
pretty quick, and it's not long before he's settled

into a nice, even stroke. I throws him a few compliments.

We stay out long enough for a good paddle, but not long enough to get missed back at camp. There won't be much happening anyway until 7:30 when the softball and soccer games start. Actually it's a pretty decent way to spend a half hour. There's something about canoeing in the evening like that when the sun is getting low in the sky that I gets right off on. And it's so friggin quiet, only a scattered bird doing lung exercises.

Morrison bugs me to go out on the pond, but I have to kill that suggestion because it's a bit windy out there. We stick to paddling back and forth on the river where it's more sheltered. Of course the first thing he says once we head back towards the wharf is how soon can we go out again. I can't go making too many promises because I knows when regular classes start tomorrow I'll have my fill of canoeing. Besides, I can't go giving him too many special privileges.

"We'll see," I tell him.

"How about tomorrow morning after breakfast?"

"How about we wait till tomorrow comes and then we'll see." He knows he'll have to be satisfied with that. "I'll tell you something though — for someone with two left hands you're pretty good."

"For someone with your size brain you're not bad yourself."

"You're too young to be usin razor blades." The kid is a bit too sharp for the good of his health.

At the staff meeting we have that night, after the boys are in their cabins where they're supposed to be going to sleep, Rev. Wheaton asks how he's coming along.

"Good," I says. "Don't think there'll be too much more problem with him."

He thinks that's pretty decent. Anyway, when it comes to assigning cabins to each of the staff, he's got me on the list for cabin three, so I guess that speaks for itself. What we're supposed to do is keep an eye on them, look out for any problems that might turn up, and more than anything, keep a damper on them night-time when some get the idea that's the right time to go on the rampage.

REV. WHEATON

As director of the camp, it seems to me that if there's one thing that's absolutely necessary it's for each staff member to realize from the beginning what's expected of him. If not, there's sure to be problems. I always make it a point of setting that straight at the first meeting with the staff. We have to know why we're all here. We have to get our priorities in order.

Of course it's the make-up of the staff itself that will determine just how worthwhile a camp like this will be. I'm lucky in that I have two or three who've been coming to camp with me for years now and who know the situation, but a full, competent staff is not an easy thing to come up with by any means. There's not too many willing to volunteer to spend ten days at a camp with eighty-five boys and not get paid for it. Some years, you're fortunate, you'll strike five or six really good persons and they can carry the camp. But more years you just have to take who you can get.

That fellow Strickland is one I'm not sure of. When he phoned me and asked if he could come I couldn't quite place him, although I knew he had been at camp before. I agreed to let him come along because I knew I could use another couple of junior staff, but I'm still not sure I did the right thing. I told him, like I told the others, not to get the idea he was coming just for a good time.

Sometimes it's not only the junior staff that can cause problems. I've had grown men here who I've had to ask to leave because they treat the boys too rough. Screaming at the campers and rough-handling them, no matter how bad they might be, is not something I'm willing to tolerate. They get enough of that at home, some of them.

The first couple of days, before we settle into a routine, are generally the most hectic. Chris wants to do canoeing so that's where I've put him. He should do all right, I think, with this fellow John Earle in charge. John's never been to this camp before but he told me he's instructed at a number of Y day-camps. I was lucky to get somebody with his qualifications. A couple of years ago he was a member of the province's Summer Games team, and in September he goes back for his last year of phys. ed. at the university.

Chris should work out all right. I still say there's more to that story about Chris having to go to court than his mother was willing to tell me. He's not a bad young fellow. There's something about him — his easy-going manner — that you just have to take to. Some of that he gets from his father. Although from some of the stories I've heard his father was causing the family a lot of headaches before he left to go out west. It's a shame about that man. If there'd been more work around the place, he'd have no problems in the world about getting a job. And work — I've seen him do the work of two men last year when it came time to repair the roof on the church.

There's a touch of his father in Chris in that way too. You have something for him to do and he'll do it. I didn't hesitate for a minute in asking him to come as a counsellor. And judging by just the first day I can see I wasn't wrong. He worked around that young fellow Morrison till he got him to fit right into camp. These ten days should be a good experience for Chris. I like to give the junior staff as much responsibility as they can handle. It's good for them.

I can't say that Chris hasn't disappointed me sometimes. When he gave up serving without even bothering to come and tell me, I was disappointed in him then. It's hard to find young fellows his age willing to get involved in work with the church. Being openly religious is not an image most teenagers want to have. You try to do what you can to get them interested, but you can only do so much. At St. Paul's we have a youth service once a month. The response from the young people themselves has been tremendous. But it's only once a month and most of the young people you don't see again until a month later. On top of the fact that a good number of the older parishioners are so set in their ways they'll even phone the rectory to complain about having guitars or hand-clapping in a service. You have to be a peacemaker to all kinds in this business.

CHRIS

Rev. Wheaton is not long laying it on the line about what he expects from each of the staff. There'll be lots of laughs no doubt, but he says he expects each one to carry their own weight when it comes to the instruction classes and helping out around camp. He has a way of getting his point across without sounding like he's too much different from any of the others on the staff. A lot of the meeting is taken up with trying to straighten out a schedule for the rest of camp. Someone shows up with coffee and what I likes is that even though some of us are only sixteen and some others are married with three and four kids, we're all pretty much on even terms. It seems like nobody comes off as having any more answers than anybody else. I likes having what I've got to say to count for something.

The meeting don't go on for too long because

even in the staff hut we can hear that on the other side of the field the campers are far from settled down. You got to expect that. When I was a camper we'd always give the counsellors a run for their money on the first night. Running from cabin to cabin and clobbering people over the head with pillows was the most popular activities. I don't ever remember getting to sleep much before two on the first night of camp. Now the roles have switched and I'm the one telling them to keep the noise down and no chasing each other around. And boys, I can hear myself saying, do you want to lose them flashlights, well shut them off if you don't.

As soon as I touch the doorknob to cabin three there's a scravelling to hide the flashlights. I'm expecting just as much noise from them as I do from any of the others, but when I opens the door I gets a lot more than I bargained for. There's a string of swear words that's not exactly the best thing to be hearing at a church camp.

"Boys, and what's this all about?" I yells at them, shining my light around. They're all sunk down in their sleeping bags.

Nobody will say anything first. Then one of them pipes up, "Morrison is bawling because he got the shit scared out of him, that's all."

"Shut up!" Morrison says, the words partly smothered in a pillow.

"What happened?"

"Darren was tellin ghost stories and Dave over there started to cry."

"You fellows shouldn't be tellin ghost stories."

"Why not? He don't have to listen if he don't want to. Everybody else wanted to hear them." That's got to be Darren.

"I'm getting out of here tomorrow," Morrison says.

"Why don't you move to another cabin if you don't like the company."

"I'm goin home!"

Here we go again. So much for what I said to Rev. Wheaton. "Boys will youse knock off with the ghost stories! Why can't you be sensible and tell jokes or something."

"We've already told all we knows."

"You tell us some."

"Yeah, you must know some."

I runs through about five just to keep them quiet. That's the most I can come up with at the time. I wish Tompkins was here. He'd be able to keep their dirty little minds going all night. Between my jokes some of them come up with a few more of their own, and in all I suppose it kills close to an hour and a half, what with all the talking they do besides. They want to get the low-down on where I'm from and if I have a girlfriend and all that, and I gets it straight after a while what each of their names are and where they live.

Gradually, one by one, they drop off to sleep, till just before I goes there's only two of them left talking. Even when I'm saying goodnight to them, these two are finding something new to gab about, and I can tell by the sound of things they could keep it going for a good few hours yet.

When I cross the field and open the door to the staff hut I'm practically wiped off my feet by one of the fellows chasing after another guy with a handful of shaving cream. Craig, the guy ahead, is running around all over the place trying to get away. He almost manages it too, except that I grabs a hold of him and pins his back to the floor so the other guy can do the job on him. Some of the staff are worse than the campers, not, of course, mentioning any names. I gets an even stronger reminder of that an hour later when I jumps inside my sleeping bag and finds a load of salted cracker crumbs digging into my bare legs.

Strickland is down below mumbling something about what's he going to do for ten days because the only women around are married and practically due for old-age pension. It could a been him who done it, or more likely Craig, but I'm too tired to try to find out so I hauls the sleeping bag inside out and lets all the crumbs drop down onto the middle of the floor. I crawls back into it then like it is, inside out. Strickland mouths off about the mess.

"Forget it. I'll clean it up in the morning," I mumbles into the wall.

"You're not goin to sleep yet, are ya?"

"I'm tired."

"Com'on." He uses his foot to bounce the spring above him up and down. When I don't say anything he does it again. And again.

"Frig off."

"Want a cigarette?"

"No."

"Here." He tosses one up together with his lighter.

I turns over on my back. It's just as well to go along with the guy. He'll only bug the life out of me until I do.

"I got the feeling this camp is going to turn out to be a drag," he says.

He must enjoy being a downer. What the frig was the guy expecting?

"Already Wheaton's got me doin three different jobs. And tonight at supper he sticks me with the dishes."

"Don't worry about it." We haven't gone twelve hours and already Strickland is complaining. What's he going to be like by the end of ten days.

"You know what I'd like to have now?"

"What?"

"A cold beer."

"Good. So would I. Now go to sleep."

"You drink much?"

"A bit."

"You mean you're not as soft as I thought you were."

"What's that supposed to mean?"

"You don't strike me like the type who drinks much."

"Tell my mother that."

"The night before I came, you know what I had . . . eleven Labatt's and I hardly felt it."

A bullshitter too. "Sure."

"All right, don't believe me, I don't care. I don't say you know what eleven beer look like."

"Like shit."

But I'm not in the mood for arguing with the guy. Especially over drinking beer. That's supposed to be something I came here to forget about for a while.

"Why don't you just go to sleep, Strickland? This conversation is getting boring."

Strickland is out of his sleeping bag now, standing up, his arms leaning across the top bunk. He takes another draw of his cigarette.

"Now what's your trouble?"

"You smoke up?" he says.

"Yeah, sometimes."

"I don't believe it."

"What makes you think I don't?"

"I dunno . . . you look too straight."

"Don't let it worry you, okay?"

What's the guy after — my life story? Too straight. Where do he think he came from — a Cheech and Chong movie or something? I wouldn't doubt I've smoked more joints than he's ever seen.

"Hey," he says, "don't get uptight."

"I'm not friggin uptight."

"Okay, forget I said anything. I should go to bed I suppose," he says, dropping what's left of his cigarette into an empty Coke can. It sizzles out. He hands the can to me. "What time do we have to get up?"

"Seven o'clock."

"You must be kiddin. Course I should know. The last time I got up that early was the last time I was at this wonderful camp."

15

CHRIS

Somewhere, probably next door, there's an eager-beaver counsellor whose alarm clock going off at 6:45 drills out loud enough that it rattles my ears. Fortunately for him, it's only enough to kill my sleep for a couple of seconds. It takes a dig into the sleeping bag fifteen minutes later to activate my brain. Seven o'clock. Summer days are not meant to be faced so early.

Down below, Rip Van Winkle haven't yet brought the fun of his personality to the camp. Somewhere on the bureau a cigarette must be getting impatient. I have a beautiful cure. I sets the volume on blast and pushes an old Village People tape into the 8-track. It's a bit more than your average robin singing in a tree. From underneath a pillow a voice booms out, "Shut that off!" I do, for my own sake just as much as his. I can't stand their music.

Now there's another eager beaver on the PA, polluting the air waves. He's trying to get it across to the campers that sleeping is no longer the sensible thing to be doing. A much more interesting activity would be splashing cold water in their faces in the bathroom. That's got to be going on deaf ears. The only way I ever got up when I was a camper was by a counsellor coming into the cabin and rooting me in the ribs.

Ten minutes later, after a wash and a quick run-in with a comb, I makes for cabin three, expecting nobody to be up. Awake maybe, but not up. But inside there's no less than three fully dressed bodies, each with a smiling face. Now if that's not against the laws of nature, then I don't know what is. One fellow says he's used to getting up at six and going out in the fishing boat with his father. Leonard is his name and his Island Cove accent is strong enough to wear rubber boots. The other fellows have been making fun of him because of the way he pronounces some of his words, but it don't fizz on him one bit. He hands back the two townies in the cabin just as much as they can dish out.

For the other four not-so-lively ones I lets out a general warning guaranteed to at least wake them up, if not deafen them. All I gets in return are groans for mercy. I'm quick to tell them they shouldn't have stayed up for so long last night. Morrison is one of the four, in fact he's the least lively of the lot. I'm thinking seriously about a little unscheduled trip to the centre of the field with him, sleeping bag and all. No better way to scare the sleep out of anyone's eyes. It only takes the suggestion and the three who are up are right there to get in on the action. Morrison struggles a bit at first, but it's not much for the four of us to have to deal with. Out through the cabin door, across the field to a new grass-type mattress, only just a small bit soggy.

Morrison is slow to catch on to the joke. In fact he takes to repeating some of the choice words I heard him cough up last night. I have a mind to gag the little turkey. He stands up in the sleeping bag and starts jumping back to the cabin like someone in a sack race. Partway across he stumbles and falls. When I gets to him he's bawling, and he just stays sunk to the ground like that, crying to get pity. It bugs me that he's turned into such a bloody baby again, after I thought he had changed. I practically lug him back inside the cabin and back to the bunk. So much for his early morning taste of the great outdoors.

I leave him alone to sulk his way back to being sensible. By now the others are all up and dressed. None of them think much of the way he's carrying on either.

"Go on, you big baby."

Little comments like that I figure won't exactly do much for his homesickness. I don't want him packed up and on his way to a bus stop before breakfast. "Leave him alone boys, he'll be all right."

At breakfast he's not much better. He won't eat any cereal, no boiled eggs, not even any cheez whiz toast, which is what anybody who don't get off on the main things usually lays into. I mean if you can't even slap a bit of cheez whiz on a piece of bread and eat it, then you deserve to starve. Morrison just grumbles over a glass of apple juice. He says he's got stomach cramps. The others at the table don't pay any attention to him, spending their time instead on making away with everything that looks either bit at all like food. Kellogg's would be proud. The eggs disappear like no hen will ever think about laying again. By the end of the meal the table is a mess — egg shells and limp corn flakes mixed with spilled milk. They can't be this bad at home. That is, unless they each have their own cage.

Rev. Wheaton explains a bit about the morning program — how they should check out the schedule to see what classes they have and where, and how they're all expected to show up to each one on time. Then the duty list — what cabin gets to do what after breakfast. We escape the dishes again thank heavens, and the bathrooms and the vegetable peeling. Someone up there must be on our side this morning. What we do get is the cleaning up of the grounds, which is okay because that should only take about ten minutes.

I space out all seven of them across the field and give every second fellow a garbage bag. Then it's supposed to be a simple matter of going slow and picking up everything they see that's not grass or rock or wood. Surprising how some of them like to confuse gum wrappers with rocks. When they finish I lets all of them go back to their cabin except Morrison. To go back home again is on his mind I can tell. Give him another half hour and he'll be trotting off over to the office nagging Rev. Wheaton to let him call somebody to come and get him. I've got to try and head that off if I can. After a few minutes of wasting my time trying to get him to wise up, the only thing I can think of that might make things any better is to take him out canoeing again.

"I'll go out but don't think I'm going to change my mind," he says. We'll see about that.

He don't say much this time around. I'm the one who's doing the talking. I'm trying to tell him how I thinks it's only natural for some fellows to feel homesick and how I was a bit the first time I come to camp. But what you got to do is fight it. Everything I says seems to be doing about as much good as a wet rag in the side of the head. He's not opening his mouth.

I should stick to trying to make the canoeing fun. For something different we head out on the pond. There's not much wind this morning. I know from taking canoeing lessons at camp before that it's better to stick close to shore where it's not deep. Although it's only about nine o'clock, the sun is bright and the air is close to what could be called warm. On the spur of the moment comes the idea of a swim. Morrison don't quite grab the idea. For one thing he can't swim very well he says. That's no excuse, we're only going off from shore. It's not going to be over anybody's head. No trunks, he says. Shit, I tell him, swim in your shorts, there's only the two of us. I don't actually see the place crawling with girls.

I runs the canoe upon shore, then it's off with the life jacket and clothes, and down to my underwear. Morrison is still in the boat.

"You goin to sit there like some turd?" I ask him. I don't like to call him chicken because that could louse up any chances I might have of getting him to go in the water.

"You go in first."

"What, and freeze my arse off while you watch?" To put it simply — the water around my ankles is not exactly hot springs material. "Com'on, get your clothes off."

"You go on in."

"Com'on, old man."

He's taking off his clothes and his glasses, without knowing whether or not he should be at it. In a minute he's standing up stiff, with his arms wrapped around himself.

"Com'on, it's not that cold."

"Sure. Tell me another one."

I walks the few feet back into shore. "Don't splash me," he says.

"I'm not going to splash you. I tell you what — we'll both run out together." Make it a real Bobbsey twin show.

"I told you — I can't swim!"

"Well, wear the life jacket." He decides he'll put it back on. "When I counts to three, okay?"

"It's too friggin cold."

"Morrison!"

"Okay, okay. Let me count."

So he wants to play the head Bobbsey . . .

152

that's fine with me.

"One . . ." He drags it out.

"What, are ya stuck on one or something? We don't have till Christmas. The number after one is two in case you haven't heard. Don't you watch Sesame Street?"

". . . two . . . three!"

I don't make a mad dash because I have a feeling that the turkey is going to make it to his knees and screech to a stop. But for some reason he don't. I bulldoze my way through, and once the water reaches my shorts, I'm yelling out in pain. I dives in as fast as I can so I can get all the agony over with the one time. I makes a U-turn under the water and comes back up facing in towards shore.

Morrison is actually in the water — his whole body, or as much as he can get in with a life jacket on. The turkey even seems to be enjoying it. A grin is splitting his face like he's surprised even himself.

"It's not cold once you're in it," I tell him.

"It's okay except for the three inches of ice that's formed around my nuts," he says.

I swims around a bit more and he squirms in the water, held up by the life jacket.

"Why don't you take it off and I'll show you a few things about swimming." He's not jumping at the idea. "Com'on, you're not going to drown. It's only up to your gut. Can you float?"

"Like a rock."

"Okay, I'll start by showin you how to float on your back."

He takes off the jacket. But only after a wait that's supposed to show that he's not doing it just because I'm asking him to.

"Now, I'll hold you up first . . . don't worry I won't let you go until I'm sure you'll float."

With two of my arms under him for support, and his hand holding on to one of them like a pair of vise grips, he's lying there across the top of the water. He's stiff as a piece of board, one end bent at a 90-degree angle — his head.

"Relax a bit, you're not made of lead you know. Let your head lie back in the water."

He tries it but the old head springs back up again, eyes jammed shut, as soon as any water washes around his face. He hates having his head in the water, that's half the problem. I helps him back up on his feet and gets him to try a few head-in-the-water exercises. At first he screws up his face worse than if he had swallowed a bottle of cod liver oil or something. But gradually he discovers that it won't kill him, and on about the hundredth try, the kid even opens his eyes. Progress, I think you call that.

The real test though is being able to float. Now he's eager to try it even. And although the hold he's got on my arm is still enough to cut off circulation, this time round he's doing a lot better.

"Relax, but keep yourself straight. Don't let your ass sink down."

After a couple of minutes he's doing it well enough that I can let my arms loose and draw them away from him. He's not willing to let go the hold he's got on my arm first, but with enough promises to grab him if he starts to go under, he gradually eases up.

And then, there he is — old waterdog himself, floating on his back. You couldn't pay him enough to be any prouder.

"See, it's not hard. Move your arms back and forth."

He won't say a word, as if to open his mouth would burst the concentration. He stays there like that for at least a minute.

I helps him land back on his feet.

"Nothin to it," he brags, with a grin on his face.

I tell him, "A few more lessons and I'll have you swimming."

"You really think so?"

I makes him promise me that he'll show up to his swimming classes when he has them. "And when I finds some free time later on in the week I'll help you again."

"When?"

"Maybe tomorrow, we'll see. We better get goin. We've got to be back by 9:30 and we only got ten minutes."

The paddle back has got to be a quick one. I works Morrison hard, making him put some muscle behind it and keep up a steady pace. He's so good that as we get near the wharf I think it's only right that I should whip my paddle across the water and douse him in the face as a reward. Approximately one second later he's trying to get even.

I stops when I sees the fellow Earle coming down the path. Morrison is not looking his way and keeps up the splashing long after I've stopped.

"That's a great way to break off a paddle," Earle shouts. "Whose permission do you have to be out in that canoe?" he says to me.

I didn't think I needed permission. "Nobody's," I answer.

"Then you shouldn't be out there. I thought it was understood that anybody using the canoes must first ask my permission."

"Sorry, I didn't know."

"Please don't stand up like that!" he says to Morrison who has just started to get out of the canoe. "If you don't know the right way to use a canoe then you shouldn't be in one."

Morrison, all confused, stumbles out, almost tipping over the canoe and me along with it. Another disgusted look for Earle's face.

"Sorry about that, chief," Morrison says and fakes a smile.

"Here, hand over that life jacket and paddle and get back up. What class do you have now?"

"I don't know."

"Well, hadn't you better go and find out? Move it. You're going to be late if you don't hurry it up."

Morrison runs up the path and then Earle turns to me, still in the canoe. "You're the fellow who's going to help me with the canoeing, is that right?"

"Yeah."

"Chris is your name, right?"

"Yeah."

"Well Chris, that's not a very good way to start. As I said, anyone using the canoes must first ask me. I'm responsible for those canoes and for the people using them." He's not raising his voice. Just talking quietly, like it's something I was stupid not to have known all along.

"Yeah, I guess so. I was only takin the young kid out for . . ."

"It's okay. You don't have to explain anything. Just please don't do it again. Okay?"

Okay, I'm thinking, okay. You made your point.

"Now, we have a class in five minutes. How about bringing that canoe right into the shore over there. Watch the rocks."

I push the canoe off from the wharf and I start to paddle over.

"Chris, wait . . ." He walks to the edge of the wharf, stops and leans on the paddle he's got in his hand. "When you're in a canoe alone, where do you sit?"

For the moment I don't remember exactly. I knows it's close to the middle section and more to the side. I makes a step ahead and kneels down facing the bow.

"Not there. Ahead of the bow seat, facing the stern. Okay? Ahead of the bow seat, facing the stern."

I'm not deaf. I moves again and paddles into shore. I'm holding the canoe back from striking the rocks.

"The butt of the paddle. Don't dig the blade in the gravel."

It's not that I mind being told what to do or the right way to do things, it's just that he's acting like such a friggin know-it-all. As if I don't have two clues about how to handle a canoe.

While we're on the shore with the canoe hauled up and waiting for the campers to show up, he takes the time to question me some more.

"Just how many years have you been canoeing?"

"Three."

"And where did you learn?"

"Here in camp."

"Didn't you ever take any course or any-thing?"

"No. There's nobody to give any courses like that where I comes from."

"Oh, I see. And what swimming badge do you have?"

"None. But I can swim."

"Let's hope so," he says, smiling. "So what qualifies you to be doing canoeing at this camp anyway?"

"What do you mean?"

"I mean, are you the only one they could get?"

What's he trying to say — that I don't know enough to be here? "I asked if I could do it."

"Oh, I see."

Sarcastic bastard. What the shit is so special about him?

A dozen or so campers, the first class, come bolting through the trees.

"Give us a life jacket and a paddle," one of them says.

"Hold it. Nobody gets any life jackets or any paddles. Everyone just go over there on the dock and sit down."

"I thought we was sposed to go canoein?"

"You will — eventually. Now go sit down. I have to have a talk with you first."

He gets them all to sit around in a semicircle and then he kneels down on one knee in front of them. Just to make sure they won't think they're being instructed by some half-assed jerk, he starts to talk about the canoeing awards he's got. And if that's not enough he flashes a few dozen swimming badges.

So there. Now don't that make him about the best you can get? God, it's not that there's anything wrong with having all those badges. Who wouldn't want to have them? But he haven't got to be such a jerk about it.

"Canoeing is not a difficult undertaking, but it can be very dangerous if the canoeist doesn't know how to handle his craft properly. We'll start with the basics and lay a few ground rules. First of all, a life jacket is to be worn at all times. I don't care how warm it is or how deep the water is, if I don't see that life jacket on you you're in for serious trouble. Rule number two — no horseplay. You're in that canoe for one reason — to learn to use it properly, not to fool around. That means no splashing, no trying to tip the other canoes over, no trying to tip your own canoe over. The first person I see deliberately fooling around will find himself making a quick trip back to shore."

He gives it to them full force. In fact all he does for the whole forty minutes is talk and give demonstrations. Partway through they start to get restless. And sour once they find out it'll be the next class before they'll actually get to go in the canoes themselves. It's pretty obvious Earle don't think I have much I can show them. All he gets me to do is hold the canoe while he demonstrates the proper way to get in and out. To end off, he spends fifteen minutes with them kneeling by the side of the wharf, paddling fresh air. You can just imagine how much they get off on that. If it was me, I would at least give them half the period in the canoes. Even if they did make a few mistakes, they'd learn from them. After all, that's what they come down for — to get out in the canoes, not to be talked to all morning.

After three periods I practically have his speech memorized. Then before the fourth period starts he tells me it's just as well if I go back up to camp, he can get through the class without me. Sure knows how to make a fellow feel useful. The whole morning has been the pits. And the afternoon don't turn out to be any better. He's got two more canoeing classes right after dinner, xerox copies of the other four.

At the end of the last class in the afternoon he asks me to stay around after all the campers have gone. He wants to have a "chat," he says.

"I've been thinking . . . perhaps I should give

you a few lessons to sharpen up your strokes. If you're going to work at canoeing it might be helpful to know more than the campers."

By now I feels like telling him to take the paddle he's got in his hand and shove it up his arse.

"You're familiar with the J-stroke, I take it?"

"Yeah."

"Let's just see what you can do then. I'll take the bow, you get in the stern."

The J-stroke you use to keep the canoe going in a straight line. I don't have a bad J-stroke, and I do keep the canoe straight, no way can he say I don't. What he does say though, and I might a known he'd find something to complain about, is that my recovery isn't clean enough, the blade is too far above the water.

"That's better. Not perfect, but it's better. And you know about cuts and draws, do you?" he says.

"Yes." Well, I've tried them a few times last year.

"What about sweeps?"

Never heard of them. "I knows about feathering."

"That's a relief," he says. "Paddle over by the dock and give me a demonstration."

Feathering is a way of moving the canoe sideways, like if you want to draw the canoe broadside to a wharf. It's harder to do if you're just doing it yourself with someone else in the bow. You have to put more pressure on the blade in one direction than in the other. I do the best I can under the circumstances. After all it's been over a year since the last time I tried it. Really what I do is screw it up.

As you might guess Earle is amused. I even think he really wanted me to screw it up just so he could have something to say.

"Oh well, you tried." It wasn't what he said. It was the way he said it.

I gets out of the canoe after that. I should a stepped on the gunnel and tipped the frigger overboard.

"Let's be honest," he says once he's out of the canoe himself, "you're going to need some polishing up."

"I thought I was only here to help you, not to be the expert. All the junior counsellors ever done any other year was to go sternsman and show the campers a few of the basic things. They're only eleven and twelve. You're not going to make them experts in ten days. Most of them have never even been in a canoe before."

"If they work hard enough and long enough, in ten days they can turn into very good canoeists."

"And they'll hate every minute of it."

"Chris, we're not here to teach them to have fun. And if that's the attitude you have I think I should talk to Rev. Wheaton. Probably there's another counsellor who knows more about canoeing than you do."

"Probably there is!" I says. "Probably there is! And I hope the hell you finds him." I throws the paddle on the wharf. I turns around and walks off.

So much for keeping my cool. Okay, so he's the instructor and he knows a hell of a lot about canoeing, but I'm not dumb. And I didn't come to this friggin camp to be made fun of. Where the hell do he think I could take a canoeing course? We're lucky to get a swimming instructor in Marten during the summer for frig's sake, let alone someone to teach canoeing.

It's just something that bastard is itching to do — go to Rev. Wheaton and spew out a big story about how I'm not cooperating and how it would be better if he had someone else. I can hear him now. People like that make me sick. Friggin jerk.

16

CHRIS

Later that afternoon I cross paths with Morrison again. He's running across the field on his way to the crafts hut. He slows down for half a second.

"You got to go over to the cabin. We wants to show you what we're doing. I'll be over in a minute."

He don't bother to wait for me to answer. Something must have happened to him. Where's his usual down-in-the-mouth look.

As I comes to the cabin door I'm welcomed by a dustpan of flying dirt being tossed out over the steps.

"What's going on?"

"Beefbrains, old man, come on in. You're just the fellow we wants to see. Give us your opinion now. What do you think? Think we'll end up with the most points?"

Most points for inspection is what they're talking about. Each day during the half hour before supper two of the senior staff do an inspection of each cabin to come up with the best-kept one for the day. The winner gets a banner which they nail up on the outside of the cabin. Too exciting.

"Well?"

"Pretty clean."

"Should be, we swept it up three times. What do you think of our sign?"

On the back wall on a piece of cardboard are the words "Welcome to Cabin Three," formed out in nothing less than spruce buds. Fierce.

"Not bad."

Morrison comes running back into the cabin just then. "I got some," he announces, "and a brush."

"What colour?"

"Yellow. That's all I could get."

"A bit fruity, but I guess it'll have to do. Let's get it painted. We don't have much time."

What *is* this — part two of the Industrial Revolution?

"I'm doing it," Morrison says. "I went and got the paint."

He climbs up on the bed below the sign, and taking his time, he starts dabbing each spruce bud with a bit of paint.

"What else can we do to get more points while he's at that?" Darren says. "What else can we do Beefbrains?"

"Yeah, what things did you do when you was a camper?" Leonard asks.

I don't know. Fooled around a lot. I never was in a cabin that had enough energy to work much for inspection. The fellows that won always had brainy ideas that nobody else thought of. "I spose you could make signs or something with your names on them and stick them up."

No such thing as having to encourage them. "Where can we scrounge up some cardboard? And we'll need a marker and a pair of scissors."

Two of them take off out the door and in five minutes they're back with an empty cardboard box from the canteen and a black marker and scissors.

"I got them off Crafty. But I got to have them back in ten minutes," one of them says, out of breath.

"Who's the best printer?"

Everybody agrees that they are lousy. Except Morrison. "Morrison, you any good at printing with a marker?"

"I got to finish this."

"I'll finish that. You get down here if you're any good."

Morrison seems to be shining in all the attention he's getting. It's the best time I've seen him since he came. He flattens out on his stomach on the floor and tries his own name first. Not bad, but it's a bit squish. He tears it up. He gets someone to draw two lines with a pencil on each piece of cardboard they have cut out. The second time it's a lot more even. Very good in fact, all capital letters. He does the others, and then he decides there should be a black border around each one, so he draws them in. When he finishes the boys push two holes in each piece of cardboard with the end of the scissors and tie them to the frames of their bunks.

"Looks good," I tell them.

I leave after that, because I'm still not in such a hot mood.

"Thanks for your idea," one of them says as I'm going out the door. "You come over tonight and tell us some more stories."

"Maybe."

"You better or we'll drag you over. See you at supper."

At supper I gets the full story from Morrison on how he went to swimming class and actually got in the water without anybody having to coax him. That's good, that's real good. Although I'm not half as enthusiastic as I should be.

After the meal the points for inspection are called out and the boys in cabin three come out on top with 36 out of a possible 40 points. They're really proud of themselves — wild is the word — over the fact that they won. I'm proud of them too, of the way they all pulled together and worked to win. I wish I had the interest to show it more.

Once I'm outside the dining hall and on the way to the staff hut Morrison comes up to me with the suggestion that now would be a good time to go for a swim. I don't know what it is — he's changed his tune an awful lot from before, either that or he's trying to do something to cheer me up.

"Are you for real Morrison? I had to just

about talk myself blue in the face to get you to go near the water this morning."

"That was this morning."

"What's this — and now you've grown fins or something?"

"You don't want to go?"

"I dunno."

"You should you know."

"And why is that?"

"I dunno, for a laugh." He smiles.

That little turkey is going to get it yet. "Okay, so go get your trunks on. Meet me down by the swimming place in twenty minutes, and *don't* tell anybody where you're goin."

"Right you are governor." He salutes me. There's something about that pest that I can't help but like.

He must a picked up a few things at the swimming class he went to. He walks right into the water, hardly bothering to mention how cold it is. Then onto his back. A seal couldn't a done much better.

"So, you're good enough to show off, are ya?"

"Watch, don't move from where you're standin," he says.

He gets back on his feet, sets himself about ten feet away from me, and with his hands stretched out in front of him, he plows across the top of the water in my direction. The only thing moving him is this vicious kick of his, which looks like it could probably stir up more water than a CN ferry. He jabs me in the guts with the tips of his fingers. He's back to his feet, eyes and mouth shut tight. He wipes away the water covering his face.

"You're too much Morrison, my son, too much. Does the Olympic team have your address or what?"

"Quit makin fun."

"Sorry. No, that's good. It really is. I'm not kiddin. Why don't you try moving your hands? I finds it helps when you're swimming."

"Will you lay off. I haven't got that far yet."

"Here, let me show you something. Watch."

I do pretty much the same thing he did, only instead of keeping my arms pointed straight out in front, I sweeps them down one to each side of me, just moving my arms to push me forward. "Then you can glide for a while and do it again. You can go a good distance like that. Just give it a try standing on your feet with your body bent over in the water." He tries it. "Keep your fingers pointed. Not too fast pulling back to the side . . . not bad." I gets him to give it a go across the top of the water. A bit rough, but he can do it.

I don't know, I suppose that's all right the way I'm showing him. He's still far from what you might call swimming, but he's getting there. It's a big improvement from being stood up like a frozen turd the way he was on shore this morning.

But as you might expect Earle don't think much of what I'm doing. That's the last person I wants to see show up. But it's him who comes strolling down the path, in his trunks and sneakers, and with a towel slung over his shoulder. A wonder he don't have a special extension on his trunks to make space for all his swimming badges. He's only got one on them though, but you might friggin well know that it's got to have the word "instructor" across it.

"If he wants to learn how to swim I suggest you leave it to a proper instructor. Sometimes a person who doesn't know what he's doing can end up doing more harm than good."

Is that so? Who asked you anyway? I'm not about to try to help Morrison anymore, not with braino around. And neither is Morrison interested now that we got an audience.

"We was just leaving," I tell him.

As we come into shore he goes out to his knees and splashes water up over the rest of his body, including his head. Too bad it don't soak through his skull. He does a perfect dive, of course, and then he swims in under the ropes, staying underwater until he's almost to the shore on the other side.

For sure he knows we're watching him. Once he's got a breath he starts swimming back towards us. Nothing simple like the breast stroke or the crawl. No, it's got to be the butterfly, he's got to pick the hardest stroke to show how well he can do it. I makes sure we're back-on to him before he stops.

"With proper instruction you could be doing that in six months," he says to Morrison as we start to leave.

Big friggin deal. We walk on up the path. I wonder if he's talked to Rev. Wheaton. More than likely not because Wheaton haven't give me any weird looks yet. Give Earle half a chance and I bet you any money he'll have me made out to look like some numbskull.

We go on and leave him there to impress the frogs.

"He's a pain," Morrison says.

"You're tellin me." I gives the kid the facts on exactly what happened today after the last canoeing class.

"I knew it must a been something like that. Whata ya goin to do?"

"Frig all. Wait and see what happens I spose." That's about all I can do.

REV. WHEATON

After the campfire, when John comes up to me in the office and says he's having a problem with Chris, I'm not quite sure how to take it. He says Chris has been acting way out of line. On the one hand I realize that John must know what he's talking about when it comes to canoeing. Yet I'm certainly not willing to condemn Chris without first hearing his side of the story. I'm sure I know Chris better than that.

Isn't there someone with more experience who could replace him, John wants to know. I'm doubtful. Besides, I would like to see Chris have a chance at it. Is he expecting too much? He outlines all that he plans to do during the ten days of camp, and I tell him perhaps he's not being realistic. This is not a training camp we're running.

"But if they're going to have the experience of canoeing, as you said, then isn't it better that they do it right? Do you realize the number of canoeing accidents there are each year?"

"What I'm saying is that beyond the basics, I don't see the point, John. You have to bear in mind that most of these boys are only eleven and twelve. And I don't want them pushed into a situation where it becomes a chore rather than fun for them."

"Learning something need not be a chore you know."

I don't want to get into an argument with him. "I'll talk to Chris," I tell him, "and see can't we get this thing straightened out. I would like to see him given another chance. The fellow hasn't had an easy time of it lately. To prove he can do it could mean a lot to him."

I see I'm going to have to walk a careful line in dealing with John. He has the qualifications but he probably doesn't have the experience of working with teenagers. He's only young and he tends to be a bit too sure of himself.

I'll wait and hear what Chris has to say before I decide what to do. I could be wrong, but Chris never did strike me as the type who would rebel against someone for no reason.

The kids like him, it's no trouble to see that. I haven't seen him yet but there's been two or three trailing after him. He takes good interest in the campers and to me that, more than anything, is what I look for in a counsellor. Right now he's over in cabin three trying to get them settled down for the night. He's spending a lot of his time with those boys, and they appreciate it. I'll have a talk with him first thing in the morning and get this cleared up.

CHRIS

The campfire each night can be one of the best things about camp, if the young fellows would give it a chance. But with that number of kids there's got to be so many among the crowd out to make a nuisance of themselves with their flashlights, or laughing and creating a racket. I can get off on just the fact of sitting around outdoors in the night, staring at the way the fire sends up flankers.

There was five or six songs and some jokes, and before it broke up Rev. Wheaton said a couple of prayers. For most of them then it was one mad stampede back to the dining hall for some hot chocolate before going to their cabins for the night.

About a half hour later when I shows up in cabin three the first thing I do is make a deal with them that the quicker they get undressed and into their sleeping bags, the longer I'll agree to stay. That settles them down a bit and gets out of their little minds any ideas about going out later and raiding the other cabins.

"Beefbrains, do you know how to play poker?"

"No poker."

"Com'on, old man, only for matches."

"No poker."

"What then?"

"We'll talk about girls, eh?"

"You're too young," I tease them. "I wouldn't want you fellows to get over-excited."

"Wow, too young. Knock off. Probably knows more than you do." Women killers, all of them.

"You wouldn't have to know much."

"Morrison," I says, "how would you like a fat lip to match that fat head of yours."

"Only kiddin. You probably knows a lot about females."

"That's better."

"Female dogs."

"Crack him one Beefbrains. I wouldn't take that."

He can be sure I don't. I have him squirming all over the place as I pokes and jabs my way through to his ribs.

"I know what we can talk about." It's Jason this time.

"What?"

"Who here has ever been to Disney World?"

"Frig Jason, we're not all rich like you. Where do you think we got the money to go to Disney World, old man?"

"What does your father do?"

"He teaches chemistry at the university."

"See, rakes in the dough I wouldn't doubt. Make no wonder you can go to Disney World."

"We're not rich, dummy. What about your father, what does he do?"

"He works for the forestry department."

The question goes all around. Of the five others — two of the fathers are fishermen, one sells insurance, one is a mechanic. And the other, Morrison, don't know.

"Whata ya mean you don't know?"

"I don't live with my parents," Morrison says.

"Then where do you live?"

"In a foster home," he says quietly.

Wheaton never told me that. Shit, it really surprises me. Nobody says anything for a while.

"You like it there?"

"It's okay."

"How long you been there?"

"Ten months."

"Where was you before that?"

Kids that age don't mind laying on the questions. They don't think for a minute that he might not want to talk about it.

"In another foster home."

"When was the last time you seen your parents?"

"Okay boys, that's enough questions," I tell them. "Com'on, talk about something else."

They do. But what Morrison said about living in a foster home sticks with me the whole time. I'd like to get him to tell me some more about it, only I haven't quite figured out how to go about doing it without him being embarrassed.

It must be 12:30 or later before I leaves the cabin. Some of them have gone to sleep by then, but Darren and Jason, the night hawks, and Morrison are still wide awake. They try to talk me into going over and getting my sleeping bag so I can spend the night in the cabin, but I works my way out of that one. Some other night, I promise them. Maybe tomorrow night. I needs some sleep.

Hardly two seconds after I'm outside the cabin, someone sticks their head out the doorway and calls me back. Of course it's got to be the turkey himself.

"Beefbrains?" he says, just loud enough for me to hear.

"Yeah, whata ya want?"

"We goin canoein tomorrow?"

"You want to be the one to ask Earle?"

"Com'on, never mind about him."

"I got to mind about him. I don't want to get into shit."

"We could go when he's not around."

"Like when?"

"Like early in the morning."

"Are you kiddin?"

"How about six o'clock? Are you up that early?"

"Six o'clock!"

"Okay, six-thirty. Com'on, just for half an hour."

"I don't know about that."

"Com'on. *Please.*"

He's never showed so much interest in doing

anything before, interest enough that he's willing to get up at six-thirty. Six-thirty — the kid must be nuts or something. Who knows, perhaps he never had anyone do those kinds of things with him before.

"Okay," I tell him after a while.

"Six-thirty?"

"Yeah. And all I'm goin to do is come in that cabin and shake you once. If you don't wake up that's your own tough luck."

"I'll wake up, I'm a light sleeper."

"Goodnight."

"Beefbrains . . . thanks."

"Get in there and go to sleep before I change my mind."

God, six-thirty. That's less than six hours away. I'm the one who must be nuts. I heads back to the staff hut determined that I'm going to get some sleep.

"Chris." It's Strickland, just coming out of the can. He follows me in the room and shuts the door. "Wheaton was here earlier on lookin for you. I told him you were probably in cabin three, as usual. He said he wants to talk to you first thing in the morning."

I figured as much. First thing in the morning — sounded like serious stuff. Shit.

Strickland puts on the 8-track and we both sit on his bed.

"What does he want you for?" he asks me.

"Is Earle out there?"

"He's gone to bed, the shithead. Blamed me

for messing up his sleeping bag. He's a real down-er, man. Thinks everybody should be in bed by 12 o'clock. Said it's not fair to those people who want to sleep."

"Sounds like something he'd say." I tell him the whole story of the canoeing classes and then the little incident with Morrison. "Frig, he pisses me off. Except for him this camp would be all right. I wonder what the hell Wheaton is going to say?"

"Forget about it. You'll find out soon enough."

"I can't forget about it."

"You're not goin to bed yet, are ya?"

"Yeah, I got to get up at six-thirty."

"Six-thirty? What the hell for?"

I explains it to him while I digs out the alarm clock.

"Earle would love to know about that."

"Frig off."

"Listen, don't go to bed yet."

"I got to or I'll never get up."

"I got a little surprise. It'll take your mind off your problems."

"Strickland, about the only thing that would take my mind off my problems is some broad willing to jump in that sleeping bag with me."

"It's the next best thing. Look here." He takes out his cigarette pack and flips open the top. There fitted neatly between his Rothmans are two joints.

"Man, are you crazy? If Wheaton ever caught you with that he'd have you strung up by the balls."

"Knock off. Who's goin to know?"

"Everybody, once you light one up."

"We're not goin to smoke it in here you fool. We'll go down in back of the first aid hut. That's a perfect place. I was down there today checkin it out."

"No way."

"Whata ya scared of, man?"

"I just don't think this is the right place to be doin dope."

"You're soft, that's all it is."

"Frig off."

"Yes you are. What friggin harm is a little grass goin to do?"

"I just don't want to go at it."

"I'll tell you what — we'll smoke *one*. One is not goin to get us off very much. You'll sleep like a friggin baby."

It's true, one is not going to get me wrecked, just give me a good buzz. I'm not sure, though. If anyone ever finds out, what a pile of shit would I be in then. I've got enough problems as it is.

But what I have in back of my mind, after I've gone over everything, is that Strickland is right — no one would ever know. I could use a good laugh.

"You sure you ever did it before?"

"Yes, and I told you that last night."

"Somehow I think you're lyin."

"Strickland — frig off will ya."

Strickland gets up and shuts off the 8-track. He takes his jacket from the end of the bed and puts it on.

Not that I don't have a choice. But what the frig odds. It's only going to be one joint. No one will ever know.

Strickland wets it down and lights it up in back of the first aid hut. Like he said, no one is anywhere around. It's a good size joint he's got there. You can get a good toke and keep it down for a long time. Two tokes and I'm starting to get a good size buzz off it already. By the end of the joint I can feel myself pretty well up there.

"Shit, that's good stuff," I says, holding down the last toke.

"Frig man, I'm right off. You?"

"Perfect. Perfect."

Weed usually calms me right down. I never does anything crazy when I'm smoking up, other than laugh a lot if something strikes me funny. I just likes to take it easy and take in what's going on around me. I'm getting right off on just sitting there outdoors, the wind blowing the trees a bit. And the smells too. I finds everything stronger or something when I'm high. I can smell and taste things better. And music, music seems a whole lot better.

Strickland wants to go back to the room and listen to the 8-track. He says he's got some good stone music.

"Wait a minute. Just take it easy."

"Let's smoke the other one."

I thinks about it a lot. I don't say no.

The second joint comes close to getting me wrecked. Not that I don't know what I'm doing. I can handle it. I'm not stumbling over anything. If I wanted to I could look normal. I bet, just to look at me, no one would ever say I'm stoned.

On the way back to the staff hut I catch sight of this kid running across the field in his pyjamas. It freaks me out a bit. I don't want anybody having to talk to us, especially any of the boys.

"It's okay, man, he's only goin to the can."

In the room, I'm out of my clothes and in the sleeping bag in about two seconds. Man, that feels nice. Strickland puts on a Pink Floyd tape and shuts off the light. The music is only down low, but just lying back I can hear every instrument, all separate. It's an excellent stone. For a while about the only other thing that comes in my mind is Susan. What I wouldn't give to have her around right now. I guess though it's only a few minutes before even that fades away and pure sleep takes over.

17

CHRIS

The clock erupts at six-thirty, not a second over-time. I'm awake enough to bat it back into its case so the stupid thing will shut off. In the back of my mind somewhere I knows I should be awake and getting up, but I'm in no frame of mind to start the struggle. All I can think about is more sleep.

It can only be a few seconds later when I hears my name coming through the window from out-doors. I opens my eyes, not quite able to focus my mind on what it could be, until it registers that the voice is Morrison's.

"Chris," it's saying. "Chris." The voice is low, like he don't know if he's at the right window.

I sits up in the bed. I finally realize why he's there.

"Give me five minutes," I tell him through the window.

I'm dragging my legs over the end of the top bunk, trying to come to my senses. My head is longing for another few hours on the pillow. But I got to get going. I jumps down from the bunk. Shit, it's the wrong thing to have done. The collision with the floor rocks my skull. The truth is I'm still feeling the dope a bit. That what Strickland had was potent stuff.

After all the fun of getting into jeans and a shirt, I makes my way to the washroom. Perhaps cold water in the face will help. It does, a bit. But not quite enough. I hates being strung out like this.

Outside, the sky is overcast and it's not very warm. It don't look like there'll be much sun today. Morrison is all dressed up in a turtleneck sweater and jacket and ready to go.

"Morrison, tell me, who else do you know would do this for you?"

"I can't help it if you're the only sucker around."

He scrambles to one side, laughing, just missing my fist.

"You're askin for it. Com'on, let's get goin, we haven't got much time."

"Who was the one who was goin to have to wake me up, eh?"

"I overslept."

"Excuses. Com'on, I'll race you down there."

"I haven't got the energy."

"Yawn again and you could float down like a hot air balloon." If I had enough life in me I'd catch the turkey and pound it. The joke is, he's almost right — a bit higher and I could float down.

The canoe seems to slide into the water smoother than ever. Two paddles and two life jackets and we're away. I'm starting to like it now that I've finally stopped feeling an urge to go back to sleep. Earle, how's this for a smooth recovery on the J-stroke.

Morrison is the one really getting off on it. I gets a great kick out of how much he's enjoying it, right down to the stupid grin he's got on his face. He should be a great laugh to have for a brother, although if he was part of my family there'd probably be a thousand reasons for me and him not getting along.

He wants to go out on the pond. I'm not sure, it seems to be getting more windy. Course it wouldn't be the first time out, he's got some experience behind him. Earle wouldn't think much of it but I'm not much worried now what Earle thinks.

The channel through the mouth of the river into the pond is a breeze, easier than it was yesterday because once we get out so far the wind is behind us and it takes us right through. Kneel down, I tell him, it makes the canoe more stable. The wind is blowing straight across the pond, and it seems like it's picking up a bit. The way we're paddling, right with it all the time, it's a great bit of fun. It's like a free ride. If we had something to rig up for a sail now it would be an even greater laugh.

Ochre Pond is a big one, I'd say it's close to a mile and a half across. I don't want to paddle too far because going back we'll be against the wind and that'll make it ten times harder. We're really going to have to work then.

I glance behind me and, by the looks of

things, we've gone farther than I realized. That's because of the wind. It's working up the water a lot and the farther we go the bigger the waves seem to be.

"Morrison, I guess we better turn around," I tell him.

"Naw, not yet, this is fun."

"Yeah, but we don't want to be all day trying to get back. Now stay low in the canoe and when I tell you, you paddle on the right-hand side as hard as you can."

Turning the canoe around could be the tricky part. I've got to be quick and have her side-on to the waves for as short a time as I can. I lets two or three waves pass under us until I figure it's about the smoothest water we're likely to get.

I back-paddles on my left side to start bringing her around.

"Now," I tell Morrison and he really starts digging in. He's got to give it all he's got because the wind is blowing dead on to the bow.

But no problem, I'm thinking.

Then I sees this frigger of a wave and I knows we're going to have to really give it to her to keep from getting water aboard. But even if we don't it should only mean we go back with a few pounds of extra weight. A canoe won't sink if it fills up with water.

We don't make it in time.

"Morrison, keep her steady for frig's sake!" But shit, the force of that wave is way more than I'm counting on.

And instead of leaning into it to counterbalance the force, Morrison's weight is on the opposite side.

"Watch out!"

But no way can I keep her upright. The wave plows sideways across the left of the bow and whips us up . . .

And over! Holy shit. I can't believe it's happened.

The friggin canoe is bottom up! I'm okay. I'm okay. The water is not that cold and the life jacket keeps me afloat.

"Morrison!"

I don't panic, but the problem is I can't see him right away.

"Morrison!"

I works my way around to the other side of the canoe. He's there, thank God. But something is far from right. One of his hands is gripping the side of the canoe, but the other is moving like mad through the water. His head is only just above the surface because the stupid life jacket he's got on is not done up in front. His glasses are gone off his face.

"Morrison, are you okay?"

When I gets near to him he grabs me around the back of the neck. He's scared.

"Take it easy! Are you okay?" He's dazed. He don't answer me. "Calm down for frig's sake. We're goin to be fine. Calm down!"

I got to do something to settle him down. If he'd keep still long enough maybe I could fix his life jacket. I try to haul the two front halves together to zipper them up but it's almost impossible. And he's got so much friggin clothes on it's like he's waterlogged.

"Hit my head," he says, his first words.

"Where?"

He rubs his forehead and when I holds back the hair covering it I can see a mark, long and reddish. The skin is not broken so there's no blood. The canoe must a struck him when it flipped over. Thank God it didn't knock him unconscious.

It had to hurt, though. He's not thinking sensible. He's holding onto me so tight it pains. I wants him to float on his back for a second so I can try to do up the life jacket. He won't listen to me. When I try to force him he starts to bawl. Jesus.

"Morrison, stop it for God's sake. We're goin to be all right."

"No," he moans.

"Yes we are. Now calm down." I feels like giving him a damn good shake, but who knows what that would do to his head.

We're going to be all right. I'm not panicking. I'm thinking it out as clear as I can. The canoe should stay afloat no matter what. And the shore don't seem to be that far away. If Morrison would act sensible I bet we could swim back to shore easy enough.

What I needs to do is get rid of some of the weight on me so I can move around better. If I could get some friggin clothes off. The sneakers are no problem. I force each one off with the opposite foot. The jeans I undo and it's a hard struggle but I gets out of them. That's a whole lot better.

If Morrison would do the same that'd mean he'd float that much better, but he won't even listen to me. I try to get hold of one of his legs to force off whatever it is he's got on his feet, but the fool kicks and kicks at me until I knows it's useless to be at it. He's got some kind of short rubber boots on his feet with jeans tucked inside. Make no wonder he's having trouble floating. The friggin boots must be filled up with water.

I have to get his life jacket fixed right, that's all there is to it. And I manage after a while to get the two ends of the zipper together. But no matter how hard I works at it I still can't get them to fit each other, not underwater with him moving around like that. As a last resort I ties the two cords, one coming from each side at the bottom of the life jacket, around his waist. I ties them in a knot so tight that no way can it come undone. It's some improvement. The life jacket is holding him up better in the water.

For the next few minutes all I do is float there trying to think about what we should do next. The wind is even stronger now than it was before. We'll never be able to swim with the canoe into shore with wind like that, and if we stick with the canoe, where we're going to end up or how long we're going to have to stay out here, I don't know. Where we are don't look all that far off from shore. Even with the wind blowing the way it is I think we could get there in perhaps ten or fifteen minutes by swimming together. The longer we wait, the farther from shore we're going to be. And I'm thinking that with Morrison's head like it is, the quicker we get ashore the better.

Morrison is settled down a bit from the way he was first, but he's still no help in trying to decide.

"Your head hurt?"

"Yes, it's poundin and poundin."

"Think we should head for shore?"

"I dunno," he whines.

"Are you cold?"

"Freezin."

The chill in the water does get to you after a while. I was too frightened to feel it first but now I do.

"I think we should try it. Moving should warm us up."

"You're going to have to help me."

"First we get you out of those stupid rubbers."

Finally he has sense enough to let me haul them off.

"Any better?"

"Yeah." That's all I can get out of him.

I have to make a decision pretty soon. I knows there'll be no changing plans if we head for shore. Once we leave the canoe it'll drift away and we might never be able to get back to it again. I keep remembering stories I've heard about people who have left overturned boats to swim to shore but never made it. Of course they couldn't a had life jackets. When I thinks about it I can't see how we can go wrong. The life jackets will keep us afloat even if it takes an hour to get there. It's better than drifting across to the other side of the pond and nobody knowing where to look. Once they discover us missing one of the first things they'll do is head this way, especially when someone finds that a canoe is gone from the shed.

"Okay Morrison, we're goin to swim to shore. We'll stick together, so don't worry. But you're going to have to work. Don't go gettin slack on me. Remember what I showed you about swimming on your back and moving your arms? Well, that's all you got to do.

"You ready?" He nods. We push away from the boat and onto our backs. That's the only way I can move because of the way Morrison's got his arms so tight around my neck. We make a fairly good start, nevertheless. We're both kicking and doing the backstroke with our free arms. With the wind blowing up the water like it is I knows it's bound to be slow going. But if we can keep a steady pace, then there should be no reason that we won't do it, eventually.

The canoe drifts away.

I try to keep talking to Morrison to keep up his spirits. He's scared still and he's in no mind to try to cover it up.

"We're gettin there," I keep telling him. But it's slow going, I knows it's slow. And the friggin waves lopping us up and down makes it all the worse.

After about five minutes I'm almost afraid to look over my shoulder to see how far we've gone. It must be a fair distance. My arms and legs are feeling the strain now, not to mention what Morrison must be going through. When I do look it frightens me because the shore seems almost as far away as when we started. We got to be moving faster than that.

If I could come up with another way of swimming. But the thing is, with two together there is no other way. We'll just have to keep going like we are.

Morrison is getting more and more tired. The stupid coat he's got on under the life jacket is no help. He looks to be in real misery.

"Stop for awhile," he says.

"We can't do that, the wind will take us back out again."

"I'm too tired to move," he groans.

"You have to."

"I can't. My head hurts. I'm dizzy."

"We got to keep goin.'"

He tries again and him trying makes me work all the harder. I begin to keep time with the arms moving. "Stroke . . .," I says, "stroke . . . stroke . . ."

He's working and we've got to be making progress. I looks to shore again and it looks like we are closer. We got to be. There's no way we can't be getting closer.

"Stroke . . . stroke . . . stroke."

But his arm is getting weaker all the time. Eventually all he does is flop it back over his head and let it drift down alongside of him.

"Change sides and we can use our other arms."

We do that and I starts again with new life.

But Morrison is no better.

"Com'on." I have to be hard on him.

"I can't. I'm dizzy."

"You got to!"

Again he tries, this time as hard as he can.

A few seconds of a steady pace and then his arm flops down and don't return. His head swings down sideways in the water.

He's passed out.

"Morrison!"

I grabs a hold of his head and hauls it upright. I wipes away the water. He couldn't take the strain. His head, it must be where he hit his head.

The first thing that I can think to do is check to see that he's breathing. He's got to be just unconscious. It can't be anything friggin worse than that.

He is breathing, thank God.

I puts one arm under his chin and tries to swim that way using a side stroke. It's so friggin hard, but I can't give it up.

All I can think about is can he die. Where he got hit on the head, can the cold water and all that struggling he went through, can that kill him?

My God, I'm thinking, I can't let that happen.

I'm in no condition myself to move very fast. And the friggin wind won't slack for a minute.

After a while I gets so tired I got to change positions. I try wrapping my legs around his waist and doing the backstroke. It could be working. I'm almost too friggin tired to care.

I looks over my shoulder and I can't even tell anymore how far we've gone. I hardly fuckin cares.

"Morrison, keep breathing, for God's sake."

I stops swimming to check on him. I think he's okay, just unconscious.

I saw on TV once you could huddle together to keep warm. Perhaps he needs more body heat. Perhaps I better give up trying to swim with him. Shit, I don't know what it is I should be doing.

I puts my two arms under his and squeezes into him. His head is against my shoulder and out of the water.

"Morrison, don't give up on me, for frig's sake."

I'm not crying. I'm so friggin miserable the only thing I can do is pray to God to get us out of this.

"Help!" But it can only be useless screaming.

It's hard to give a shit anymore what happens. I holds onto him with all my strength and shuts my eyes. We could be drifting for ever.

I don't know how long we're there like that. It could be ten minutes. It could be half an hour.

I just knows that one time as we're drifting and I'm facing the shore I sees the shape of a canoe and two men paddling towards us. They come closer. It's Earle and Rev. Wheaton. The crying I'm doing must be in thanks.

When they reach us I help them get Morrison aboard. It's not easy. Neither is it easy for me to lunge up and try to spread my weight across the canoe.

Earle checks on Morrison. He's still breathing. Earle turns the canoe around with no trouble at all and takes us towards shore.

18

REV. WHEATON

As camp director, being the one responsible for eighty-five boys, you always have it in the back of your mind that something like this could happen. You take as many precautions as you can, but you prepare yourself for the worst. Then you thank God that your strongest fears have not been realized.

The boys are okay now. For a while it looked like it could have been much more serious, especially for young Morrison, but according to the doctor, with plenty of rest he should be fine. The doctor wants to keep him in the hospital for at least three or four more days. The head injury combined with the chill he received could have been fatal had he been in the water for very much longer. He wasn't all that healthy to begin with, the doctor told me.

Chris only had to stay in overnight for observation. I've decided that the best thing for Chris to do is return home to Marten when the hospital releases him. He wouldn't fit in very well at camp now. To let him work with canoeing is out of the question.

When I go to pick him up I check on David. He's awake and talking. It looks like there won't be any complications. A child welfare officer has shown up at the hospital and I have to try to explain to her as best I can the circumstances of the accident.

Chris insists that he doesn't want to visit David's room before we go. He says he spent a long time with him last night. I don't argue but I would have thought it only considerate for him to go and say goodbye.

The trip to Marten will take two hours. If Chris had his way he would take the bus home, because he doesn't want to have to face me for such a long time. But I insist that I drive him there. I haven't shown him any anger yet and I don't see what it would prove at this stage, but I do intend to get an honest explanation for what happened. It was carelessness on his part and he knows it. It might be argued that he's suffering enough now just having to live with his conscience. But I think if he could talk it out it would help to settle everybody's mind. Keeping all his feelings concealed is certainly no solution.

He's more nervous than I've ever seen him before. He's trying hard to look normal, but it's not working. It's a far cry from the way he usually acts. He thinks, I suppose, I'm going to lecture him.

"Chris," I try to tell him, "you might as well settle down. It's going to take us two hours to get there."

He smiles weakly but doesn't say anything. I'll

give him time because I think he should be the one to bring up the subject he knows we both have on our minds. It takes another ten minutes but finally he does gather up enough nerve.

"I guess you're pretty mad at me?"

"I'd be crazy if I wasn't."

He waits for a while, then he says, "It was a stupid thing I done."

"We should be thankful it wasn't more serious."

There's another long pause.

"I guess Earle was right. I guess I am pretty dumb when it comes to handling a canoe."

It's probably the easiest thing he could find to blame it all on. But he can't expect me to accept that. "I always thought you could handle a canoe fairly well."

"Earle didn't think much of me, though, did he?"

"That's not what caused the accident."

"You don't think so?"

"Am I right?"

He doesn't answer. He looks more upset than ever.

"Poor judgement and carelessness are two reasons. Isn't that right?"

"I guess so."

"What baffles me is why you went out on that lake in the first place. You must have known that strong wind can be tricky. And then to have someone with you who couldn't swim. John said you knew he couldn't swim. Was that true?"

"Yes."

"Then what made you go?"

"I dunno," he says. He knows I'm waiting for more. "I guess I just wasn't thinking right. I was being dumb. As usual."

"Now Chris, did I ever say you were dumb?"

"Well I'm not exactly Einstein, now am I."

"I think all you're doing is looking for excuses."

Perhaps you could just label it foolhardy. When you're growing up you take some ridiculous chances sometimes and not think twice about them. That's not a sufficient explanation for what he did just the same. It was someone else's life he was fooling around with, and at sixteen I would have thought he had more common sense than that.

"What do you think your mother is going to say?"

"If she's anything like what she was when I left home then I won't hear the end of it for six months."

This attitude of his is beginning to rub me the wrong way. "Chris, my son, it's not something that you should forget about in a couple of days you know. Don't you realize that someone almost lost their life on account of you?"

"I knows that."

"Well?" He doesn't answer. "Well?"

"You don't understand." And he leaves it at that.

I don't know. In some ways I'd like to pity him. I know he hasn't had it easy at home. But I can't see going easy on him either. This is serious business we're dealing with here. It's not something you can overlook and say he's learned a lesson and end it at that.

"You know what I think?" he says after I let him alone for a while longer.

"What's that?"

"I think I should go away somewhere and get a job. Get out of Marten altogether."

"Chris, you're not even finished school."

"At the rate I'm going I never will be."

His mother has told me about the fact that he failed his grade ten. "And who's to blame for that? You know yourself it's not because you can't learn. Perhaps you're just not working hard enough."

"Now you sound like my mother."

"You ever think she could be right?"

"I don't want to talk about school. I've had enough of that already." He turns and stares out the side window.

"You mean you don't want to face up to it." He doesn't say anything. "Isn't that right?"

"Face up to what — that I'll never be any good in school compared to Jennifer? It's not exactly heaven you know to have yourself compared to some brainy sister who never gets a mark below A."

"There's a big difference between A's and failure."

"You don't understand."

"Understand what?"

"Never mind. You don't understand."

It's obvious to me that the boy is just not trying to make sense. He's looking for pity. I'm sorry but I'm just not the one who's going to give it to him.

"What you're looking for is someone to say how sorry they are for you. Isn't it? Well, that's not going to do you much good. Face up to it — nobody ever got very far by sitting on their rear-ends and saying what a rotten life they got. In a few years you'll be out on your own. Then who will you have to blame it on?"

I have to force myself to stop. I'm getting mad with him and that's one thing I vowed I wouldn't do. It kills any chances I might have had of him opening up to me, but there it is. I don't know I'm sure what to make of Chris. I thought I knew him better than that.

CHRIS

I was glad enough when we finally reached the turn-off to Marten. Rev. Wheaton wouldn't stop digging at me for answers. I didn't know what to say to him. If I told him the whole story then what kind of fix would that have put me in. I knows I should have in a way because Rev. Wheaton is one person who got a right to know. I knows I friggin well nearly got somebody drowned.

I let Wheaton down. He let me have the responsibility without any questions asked and I let him down. He should know I don't feel very good about that.

And I couldn't feel any worse than I do about what happened to Morrison. Just imagine if Morrison hadn't recovered or something. I never slept any more than two hours last night thinking about that, I'm sure I didn't. But I got to have more time to think this thing out. My mind is so friggin confused. And Rev. Wheaton had no right to blow off at me about school. Nobody can ever see anything my way.

It's one o'clock by the time we turn into the driveway. When we get to the back door it's locked, which is strange. Unless Mom is gone shopping or something. I should have a key somewhere in the knapsack.

Once I've dug it out I unlocks the door and drops the gear down in the porch. I can hear someone inside and the TV on. That's even stranger. Perhaps Jennifer didn't have to go to work today and the door has been locked since last night. There's nobody in the kitchen. Perhaps in the living room. But just as I'm about to look in there Mom walks out from the hall.

"Chris, what in the world are you doing here? Camp can't be over yet."

"How come the door was locked?" I ask her.

"I don't know. Jennifer must a locked it by mistake when she went to work. How come you're back? Is there something wrong? Are you sick?"

"May I come in?" Rev. Wheaton asks, looking in from the porch. It's odd to me that he should have to ask. Usually that's the first thing she would a done would be to invite him in. When he does come in we look at each other like neither of us knows who should be the one to tell her what's happened.

Then Rev. Wheaton speaks up. "Chris, perhaps I could speak to your mother alone first. Is that all right with you?"

It don't make any difference to me. For sure I'll be locking horns with her later on. "I'll take my stuff in the bedroom and unpack it."

I makes a move to go out in the porch, but all of a sudden Mom says, "Chris, can you go down the store and get something for dinner. I didn't have chance to get my groceries yesterday. Pick up some pork chops and some milk." She gets her purse off the kitchen counter.

"Where you goin?" she asks me.

"I have to use the bathroom first."

"I've just washed the floor in there. Can't you wait till you gets back?"

I just goes on past her into the hall as if I didn't hear the stupid question she asked me.

When I gets to the bathroom, the floor in there don't seem to have been washed at all. What's going on? I'm just about to turn around to yell out to Mom when a noise in the spare room stops me. The spare room is where Jennifer's got her sewing machine set up. But Jennifer is supposed to be gone to work. Perhaps it's just my imagination. I figure I should open the door to make sure.

I looks inside and there don't seem to be anything, until, just when I'm about to close the door, a reflection in the mirror catches my attention. I'm looking but I don't believe what I sees. It's the reflection of a man, a man I recognize. Frank Osmond is standing up behind the door.

What the hell is he doing in that room? I just stares at his reflection. All kinds of explanations run through my head — like it must be trouble with the radiators or with the electricity or something — until it strikes me that I'm thinking too simple.

Jesus, it can't be anything to do with Mom. I don't want to even think about that. But why the hell is he hiding?

And there's got to be some reason for her not wanting me to go down the hall. When I walks back out in the kitchen and looks her in the face it hits me twice as hard. She's starting to cry. God, Mom, you got to be kidding.

"Chris, wait!"

Forget it. I takes off past her and Wheaton, out the back door and out onto the friggin road. I hardly got a clue where I'm headed. Hell, I'm thinking, what the fuck's going on?

I'm cutting across a field and heading towards the wharf. I looks over all the boats tied up there and I makes a jump into the one easiest to get clear and unties her from the wharf and her mooring. There's tow-pins and oars and that's all I needs. I rows out past the wharf and the rocks. Past the point. I'm rowing all the time.

My head is all frigged up. There's so many things cramming inside for attention that I have a mind to jump overboard or some friggin thing. I still can't believe that about Mom. There must be some other reason for him being there. But I can't think of any other explanation that's sensible. If it wasn't that, then what the hell was she trying to hide?

First the accident and now this. God, it's a wonder Morrison is not dead. I thought a lot about that kid. When I went to see him in the hospital I told him I was sorry, but he said he never blamed me. He said he's going to be all right. But he don't know the whole story. Nobody does only Strickland. That fuckin Strickland . . .

And I shouldn't even be blaming it on him. Come right down to it and it was all my own friggin fault. If I had a mind of my own instead of letting myself get talked into everything all the time, then that friggin accident might never have happened. Fuck, if I had any sense I would a seen it was going to be different than getting stoned for a laugh on a Saturday night when I got nothing better to do.

Even the one who I thought might show some sympathy turned against me. I might a known even Wheaton wouldn't try to understand. I knows I couldn't expect much, but he didn't have to go getting on my back, just like everybody else. And it's not pity either I'm looking for, so it's no friggin good for him to say that it is.

I knows what the hell I'm going to do. Clear out and take off somewhere. Get away from Marten altogether. There's enough stories around here now about me to fill a friggin book. I don't know where the hell to go is the problem. Maybe out to Alberta with the old man. Then perhaps he don't want to see me either.

Perhaps I'll end up in reform school. In some ways I hope the frig I do. At least that's one place someone will take me in. That's a laugh. The court case about the stupid windows is coming up soon. Perhaps the magistrate will have the sense to fire me off to reform school until I gets enough money to fuck off somewhere on my own.

19

CHRIS

When I finally comes in off the water it's after supper. I was out there close on six hours. I spent most of those in a sheltered place called Birchy Cove. I even picked some mussels, made in a fire, and roasted them. I didn't get much straight in my mind, but at least I was able to settle down a bit. I headed back in when I figured I had enough of being alone. No matter how miserable I gets I'm not much good by myself for very long.

At seven o'clock I'm doing something I haven't done in a long time — knocking on the back door at Tompkins' place. It feels strange when Steve's mother shows up to open it, because before when I'd go there I used to just barge on in.

"Is Steve home?" I ask her.

She's surprised to see me. "My, a stranger. Come in. Come in," she says smiling. And in the next moment, "Have you been talking to your mother? She phoned this afternoon looking for you. She sounded upset. She said for you to call right away if you came here."

"I was talkin to her not long ago." A lie, but that's all I can say.

"Steve is downstairs in his bedroom. Go on down if you like."

I've been down there a thousand times, but this time it's different. I even knocks on his door, although it's partway open. It sounds like he's drying his hair.

"Chris . . . what the frig. I thought somebody told me you was in camp."

"I was."

"Well . . . come on in. I just got outa the shower." He shuts off the hair dryer.

"I didn't come for long."

"Whata you been doin? How come you're back?"

"It's a long story."

I don't know if he expects me to tell him or not. I feels pretty dumb just standing there looking at him. It's not the same as when we used to hang around together. That was only a few weeks ago, but it seems a hell of a lot longer.

"Where you goin tonight?" I ask him.

"Nowhere special. Over to Mike's. We might go down to the beach after, I dunno. It's all according if Cathy can go or not."

Sounded pretty certain to me.

"Comin with us or what?"

"I dunno."

"Why not?"

"I dunno."

I do know as a matter of fact. I'm the one who

quit being friends with him, like I had better things to be doing. If I was him I probably wouldn't feel any too happy about me showing up like this.

"Listen," I says to him. I should at least be able to get this much straight. "This what happened last month, I'm sorry about all that."

"Forget it."

"No, I means it. It was a friggin rotten way for me to be carryin on." He looks at me. "Never got me very far. To court, that's about all." I'm trying to laugh.

"I heard about that."

"What did you hear?"

"That you was in on that racket about the broken windows."

"That mightn't be true."

"Don't you know?"

I try to explain to him about that night, how I just wasn't in too much of a condition to know exactly what I was doing. "I came home plastered."

"Your old lady find out?"

"She was there to meet me."

"And you're still alive?" We both laugh.

"It was my own fault."

"You should a been more careful. So what did your old lady say?"

I makes a slit with my hand across my throat. "Had me paintin the friggin house from top to bottom for a week. Just about cleaned out Cooper's stock of paint."

"Fierce," he laughs. He puts on his shirt.

"Goin over to Mike's or what? We might get a few beer."

"I don't think so. I'm not in much of a mood for drinkin. I think I'll go somewhere else."

"Where?"

"I dunno."

"Is there something wrong? When was you ever *not* in the mood for drinkin?"

I just grin at him.

"Something happen up to camp?"

"Maybe. You really want to know?"

"Yeah, sure. Don't you want to tell me?"

I do. I have to talk about it with someone. I gets up to close the door.

"God, it can't be that bad, old man."

I spews out the whole thing, right from the beginning of camp. The smoking up, the whole bit. It do feel better having got it off my chest.

"So how's the kid now?" he asks when I finish.

"He's goin to be okay."

"I guess you was lucky. So did this guy Strickland get the boots?"

"He's still there, I spose. I didn't let on to Wheaton about the dope. Think I should have?"

"I dunno. I guess that's up to you."

"Would you?"

"I dunno. I guess I would never a smoked up in a place like that in the first place."

That just about sums it up all right. Tompkins would a told Strickland to frig off somewhere.

"That's quite the load of trouble to be in," he says.

"And I got to go to court yet too, the first week of September."

"Don't let it get to you. In another couple of weeks you'll be back to school. That'll sure as hell take your mind off it."

"I have my doubts if I'm even goin back," I tell him.

"You're quittin?"

"Thinkin about it."

"Man, I wouldn't do that if I was you."

I figured that's what he'd say. "You didn't fail, remember," I remind him.

"Shit, fail, what odds about failing. Lots of people fail."

"I got no interest in school."

"There's lots of reasons for goin back."

"Yeah, name one."

"Susan Murphy."

"Knock off trying to be Mr. Cheerful. All I needs now is leatherhead on my ass."

"She's not even goin out with him anymore."

"She's not? Since when?"

"Since two weeks ago. I figured you'd be the first one to know."

"Too busy smashing out windows. No foolin around now, is that true? You're just bullshittin me."

"No, I swear that's the truth. And she haven't started goin out with anybody else either. I tried to lay the makes on her the other night but she wouldn't have nothin to do with me. Maybe it was because I had my other arm around Cathy at the time." He grins. "She even asked about you."

"She did? Now that's bullshit."

"Yeah . . . I mean no . . . no kiddin, she did. I told her you was in camp, probably jackin yourself off thinkin about her."

"You frigger." I rams him with my fist. "Knock off."

He laughs his way over to the other side of the room and gets his jacket. "Com'on, goin out or what? We might run across her if we're lucky."

"Let's go," I says. Tongue almost hanging out.

For a minute all I can think of is that. I'd really like to forget everything else. But then there's that other thing lying there in the back of my mind.

"Wait, maybe I won't."

"Now what's wrong?"

"I guess I should phone the old lady."

"Well, go ahead and phone her. You knows where the phone is, you used it enough times."

He don't know what's going through my mind. That's one thing I can't tell him.

"Steve, is it okay if I stays over here tonight?" I ask him.

"Sure, why not."

We go upstairs and while Steve waits I phones Mom. First when I says hello she sounds really upset. She keeps saying how relieved she is to hear from me. I don't say much except that I'm staying over to Tompkins for the night. She tries to get me to come home, she wants to talk to me she says, but I just tell her I'm going out somewhere with Steve and I won't have time. She tries to get me to promise to come over the first thing in the morning. I don't say much except, "I'll see."

Just what the hell do she expect. I says goodbye and hangs up while she's still talking. That's a pretty ignorant thing to do I know.

After we leave the house, we take off over to Mike's place. The aunt he lives with gives me a hard look when she opens the door. She invites us in but we just wait in the porch for Mike to get his coat and stuff on. When we get outside, Steve talks him out of getting any beer, saying he wants to save his money till tomorrow night. Mike don't need that much convincing because he don't drink much anyway. That's pretty decent out of Tompkins to do that. I wouldn't enjoy beer tonight.

From what I can tell the two of them have their girls lined up already. Apparently Steve is pretty hot with this Cathy Delaney and Mike's got this other one he hangs around with. When they meet them down by the intersection, it makes me feel a bit out of place. And I can notice how Tompkins is trying to cover it up to make it seem like it don't matter that I'm the odd one out. He figures we should go on down to the beach, perhaps Susan is there is what he's thinking.

I hope she is. I could use a bit of new scenery. When we get there Tompkins starts walking all around and it's pretty obvious what it is he's trying to do. She's not there though. And now he's willing to drag everybody back up out of it again, just for my sake. I hauls Tompkins to one side and tells him to forget it, quit trying to be the nice guy. I'll make myself scarce for a while and come back later on. Perhaps I'll run across her somewhere else.

I never thought I would really, but halfway back up the path who the shit should I almost bang into but her. It's got to be more than just a fluke. Perhaps somebody told her they saw me go down to the beach. She's with Maureen and another girl and they're all running like they're late for something.

"Come here for a minute," I calls out to her, as if it's the most logical thing in the world to be saying. The two others just go on.

"Hi," she says.

"Why the rush?"

"No special reason."

"I heard you was askin about me?"

"I was? . . . Yeah, I guess I was. I was just wondering where you were all the time, that's all. I haven't seen you around."

I didn't actually figure she was very desperate to know my whereabouts. "Nowhere much."

Then we start our regular period of silence.

". . . I guess you've heard a few stories?" I ask her.

"A few."

"About the windows?"

"Yeah."

"I figured that." And here this great conversation stumbles to a dead stop.

"I guess I better get going." She turns to leave.

"I'd still like to go out with you sometime," I tell her. Fuck it, I might as well go all the way with it if I'm going to look stupid.

She turns back.

"And I'm not drunk this time either."

She laughs. But goes on a bit farther.

"I would . . . no kiddin."

She stops and looks around again. "Like when," she says.

"Like how about right now."

That catches her by surprise. It leaves her hanging there, thinking, almost smiling.

"Let's go somewhere for a walk."

"I can't leave Maureen and Cheryl."

"Sure you can."

"I don't know if I should or not."

Well, I can make up her mind for her if she'll let me. I walks over to where she is and takes her hand. What have I got to lose?

"Com'on, they'll know you're with me."

She don't argue. In fact I think she gets a kick out of it. It never pays to be too slack.

Shit, do I ever get off on Susan. I always did. Now the girl I had carved out in my mind is closer to me than she's ever been before. I got every reason to be excited.

I figure the first thing I should do, though, is set her straight on this window business. I don't come out of the story with much of a halo, but I think she understands a bit about how I got mixed up in it. She says she always thought Stan and that bunch were a bit sick. I'm not about to argue.

It's really good having someone who tries to understand how you feel. First Tompkins and now her. Tompkins might make a great friend but Susan has several added advantages, two of which I can't keep my eyes off.

This first time being alone together lasts longer than I would ever have dreamed about a few weeks ago. It sure beats pissing in leather-head's helmet. I even tell her about that. It was a bit gross I know, but I figure if I'm truthful with her, she's going to appreciate it. She does. And when I walks her home, it's like we've been going together for weeks or something, the way we're joking around so much. It all ends up with the best kissing session I've had in ages. I can hardly wait for the next installment.

Susan is quite the girl. She's got to be to take my mind off everything for so long as she does.

MOTHER

There's no easy way around it. It's got to come to a face-to-face meeting with Chris. And I got to explain things and hope that he'll at least try to understand.

The last thing in the world I wants to do is hurt him.

I quit my job. I told Frank last night on the phone that we just have to stay away from each other till I gets it clear in my mind what it is I'm going to do. I've got to make up my mind one way or the other about all this.

Chris don't know either that his father is coming home for two weeks. He never give me chance to tell him that, he tore out of the house so fast.

I don't know for the life of me what I'm going to say to him. There's just not going to be any way he'll understand what I've been going through these last couple of months with Frank.

I knows that perhaps it haven't been easy for him with his father gone, especially where he was so close to him one time. Rev. Wheaton said he thought that was the reason for some of the problem with him. I don't know half Rev. Wheaton said, to tell the truth. After Chris went tearing through the door I couldn't keep my mind on what it was he was trying to tell me. About the accident up to camp, I got that much. But what he was saying about Chris's attitude and how he seems to have changed, there was no way I could take it all in. I had to ask him to come back some other time. He said he thought he should come over when Gord gets home from Alberta. I told him yes, probably that was the best thing.

It's only a half hour or so after Jennifer leaves for work that Chris shows up. I didn't expect him this early.

"Where's my knapsack?" he says.

"I put it in your bedroom."

He goes on past me to his room. I ask him if he's had any breakfast.

"Yes," he says.

In a minute I follows him to the bedroom, but

the door is closed and locked. I've got work I can do in the kitchen, a pie I wants to get made. Perhaps if I gives him chance, he'll be out after a while.

An hour passes and he's still not come out of the bedroom. Perhaps he's gone back to bed. I don't want to disturb him if he is.

When 12 o'clock comes I calls out to him to come to dinner.

"I'm not hungry," he tries to tell me.

"It's pork chops and mushrooms." That's the best meal he likes.

"I'm not hungry."

He's only trying to put off what he should know has got to come. "Come on out, I've got something to tell you about your father."

"What is it?"

"Come out here."

Before too long his curiosity gets the better of him and he's in the doorway between the hall and the kitchen.

"What about him?"

"He phoned and said he's comin home next week. Isn't that good news?"

"For how long?"

"Two weeks."

"And he's goin back again?"

"He wants to see what the chances are of gettin a job here."

"If he goes back then I'm takin off with him."

"He might want the both of us to go."

"Well, for sure you won't be goin."

"I don't want to."

"No, and that's for sure."

He's starting to poke at me. I suppose I've got to expect that much. "Sit down to your dinner." It's all on the table ready to be eaten. "Com'on, sit down."

I don't think his stomach can resist the smell. He goes to the bathroom to wash his hands and he comes back in the kitchen. He's uneasy sitting there. It's five minutes of silence to the time he's finished what's on his plate. He drinks another glass of milk and gets up to go back into the room.

"Wait for dessert."

"I don't want any."

"It's blueberry pie."

He keeps on going down the hall. I gets up from the table to follow him before he's got time to shut the bedroom door.

"Chris, you might as well say it and get it off your mind. It's goin to have to come out sooner or later."

He's sitting on the bed looking at me. "Is that all you can say?"

"You shouldn't try to hide how you feels . . ."

"Good God, you must know how I feels!"

I hates it when he yells like that. He turns away from me and looks at the floor. I knows what's going through his head.

"What do you expect me to do," he says, "ask you in plain English what the frig that fellow was doin in the house?"

It's not right the way he's shouting. "I'm sorry. Chris, he only come in to talk to me."

"Tell me another one. What the hell was he doin hidin away in the spare room then?"

"I didn't know it was you who was at the door. It could a been anybody. I thought it would be better if nobody found out he was there. You knows the way people talks."

"Sure," he says.

"Chris, I'm not making any excuses. Perhaps it *was* wrong." He turns his eyes towards me. "I don't want to hurt you. I loves you too much."

"You got a sick way of showin it!"

No, I don't want to hear that. And the way he said it I can't stop myself from crying. I can't stay in the room any longer.

"I'm sorry," he says after it's too late. "I didn't mean that."

He follows me out to the hall.

"Mom, I'm sorry I said that."

When I turns and sees him standing up by the door to his room I can't help but see that he deserves to know more than what I've already told him.

"Chris, there's nothin I can say that's goin to give you all the answers you're lookin for. Frank come to the house to talk to me, that's all and that's the truth."

It's still not enough, I knows. He's looking for more than that.

"Chris, he's after me to get a divorce from your father. But you knows yourself I wouldn't want to see the family split up. What's going to come out of all this, I just don't know. When your father gets home some decisions are goin to have to be made. That's all I can say."

He's old enough to be able to accept that. I just don't want to hurt him any more than I have to, that's all.

20

CHRIS

It's been a good while since we done this — gone in the woods together fishing, me and the old man. The beginning of September is a bit late for trout but we decided we'd give it a try anyway. The old man said it'd be good just to get away. I would a took the 12-gauge, only the duck season is not open yet.

Dad got back from Alberta on Friday, just as the Labour Day weekend was starting. This is Sunday and a lot of talk has gone on in between. Some of it out in the open. A good bit more I daresay must a been done when I wasn't around, because I can notice a lot of difference in the old man since first when he showed up. I haven't said much to him, other than some things about me, so it must a come from Mom if he knows it at all. I hope she had the guts to tell him, because I sure as hell don't want to be the one.

The first day when he got back he didn't open his mouth about me having to go to court because he was just too glad to be home to spoil it for anybody. He come back with all kinds of stories about his job and what it was like living up there. He says the only good thing he sees in it for a married man like himself is the money. Only for that he would a been home long before this. And it's only the money that's going to take him back if he goes. I can see just how bad he wants to stay.

On Friday night a whole bunch of people showed up at the house to see him. He brought out a bottle of Alberta whisky and planked it down in the middle of the kitchen table. There was lots more liquor besides, but nobody ended up getting very drunk. About ten o'clock Mom put on a scoff. The old man said he'd been dying for a good meal of fresh fish and potatoes since he left and that's just what he got, some Bert Critch sent over after he heard that the old man was on his way home. It looked to me like Mom cooked enough for half of Marten, but it all got put away somewhere or other. Even old lasagna-face herself, Jennifer, had a taste. Bakeapple jam then on fresh bread to top it all off. It was a real Newfoundland feed.

The old lady, everybody, was having a good time. After the meal then Dad got the whole works of them out on the floor. They had to have a few dances, he said, or it wouldn't be much of a time. It was no stopping then with the music till after three. By the looks of things he's more of a Newfoundlander now than what he was when he left. It must a been close to daylight by the time the last person went out through the door.

Too bad, except for what some of us had on our minds it would have all been a great old laugh.

The old man was after me and Mom to have a dance the whole night. I wasn't sure I wanted to, but I did in the end just because he was keeping on after me so much. It was a real frig up. I knew it was going to be even before we started. We couldn't keep in step and anyway the old lady was half ready to bawl all the while we was on the floor. I guess I felt kind of sorry for her.

I knew sometime on Saturday it was going to have to come down to a few words about the little run-in I had with the law. I told the old man all I knew about it. At least this time he listened to me. He did keep on for a while about how bad it was for me to have to go to court, but he wasn't near as mad about it as what he was on the phone that time. The more we talked, the dumber I looked for having let myself get into that bad a situation in the first place. I did sorta apologize for the whole thing. He said him and Mom are both going with me when I goes to court on Thursday.

For now, though, we got all that out of our minds. We're having a pretty good time of it fishing. We had to walk for about two miles from the road to get here, but it's worth it. Some nice size trout in this pond.

You should a seen the state the old man got into with his fishing line. He was reeling it in when the hook got caught on a stick on the bottom. I told him before that the red devil he had on was too heavy.

"Cut the line," I said.

He wouldn't listen. Too stubborn for his own good.

"What, and lose that lure?"

He hauled up his thigh rubbers and started to wade out, figuring maybe he could reach it before the water got too deep. He made it out so far and he was just about to where it was stuck, when down he goes. He lost his footing and ended up in water up to his waist. I just about shit laughing at him. He got his line clear though. He come back in sappin wet, rubbers right full of water. Serves him right.

The fire we build gives him chance to dry off a bit. Fried up like they are in salt pork, the trout soon takes his mind off it anyway. That's the best way I likes trout, fried up like that just after they come out of the water.

We're sitting around the fire waiting for the water to boil so we can finish off with a cup of tea. When it starts to bubble up in the can the old man leans over and tosses in a couple of tea bags.

I wish he wouldn't, but he starts getting serious again. He don't mention about going to court anymore, but what he wants to know is what's all this Mom's been telling him about me wanting to quit school. Tuesday school starts and I pretty well got my mind set on not going back.

"I'm old enough you know," I tell him.

"That's not the point."

"I wants to find a job."

"You won't find much with what education you got for sure."

"It's better than stickin around here."

"That's what you thinks now. Just wait till you goes out lookin for work. Who's going to hire some sixteen-year-old kid that's only got grade nine? I thought you had it in your head to get your grade eleven and then go to trades school or something."

"I changed my mind. Sure, you got a good job out of it and you don't have much of an education."

"It's not a good job. It's good wages but that's all that's good about it. When you're like I am you works at what you can get, not what you wants. I'm sick of it. Just look at where I had to go to find work."

"I hates school," I says. "I do, I hates it."

"So did I when I was goin to school, but if I had any sense I would a stayed there. I was thirteen years old when the old man said, okay, my son, you don't have to go anymore if you don't want to. What he should a done was kicked me in the ass and sent me there. I'd be a darn sight better off for it today."

I knows there's no sense in arguing with him. He's like the old lady now — once he starts in preaching it's just as well to shut up. Maybe I wouldn't mind going back to school so bad if it wasn't for having to face everybody with all the stories that's around about me beating up school property. Anyway, I thought the old man had it in his head for us all to pack up and move away.

"You'd have to start school here first. Even if I do get the family to move, it wouldn't be till later on the fall."

"What about Mom?"

"What about her?"

"She goin out there too if we goes?"

He turns and starts putting the mugs and stuff in the knapsack. "Who the frig knows what's goin on in your mother's mind. One minute she says one thing, the next minute something else." He goes over to put out the fire. "Anyway I'm not lettin that stop you from startin school, so don't think you're goin to use it for an excuse. I mightn't be goin back to Alberta anyway. I got to go in and have a talk with Manpower on Tuesday."

"Someone said they're goin to start work on a fish plant soon."

"Christ, they've been chewin that over for four years now."

"If it's true then maybe there'll be a job in it for you."

"You never knows."

If he did get a job then he wouldn't have to go away again. With the old man home and working that'd make the thoughts of going back to school a bit better.

Dad, I think, is looking at it the same way. "If that's the case, then the fall you be ready for some partridge huntin."

There's something, finally, that sounds like it might be worth looking forward to.

MOTHER

With Gord and Chris gone in the woods and

Jennifer at work, I'm left in the house by myself. I've got more than enough to keep me busy just the same, things I got to get done for Jennifer before she leaves for university. She finishes up her job tomorrow and then it's only a few days after that before she goes. She bought some material on sale last week for me to make her two tops, and still all I've managed to do is get the patterns cut out.

I've just had too much on my mind the last couple of days with Gord back. I wasn't sure what it was going to be like, but it's turned out to be good to have him home. For a while at least he's like his old self. The worst thing is now that's got me more mixed up than ever I was. Last week I just about had my mind made up to leave, but now I almost think I might be making away with every good thing I ever had if I goes and does that. It's only since he come home that I've been able to think about the good parts of our marriage. Not the few months before he left now, cause that was nothing more than one damn torture. But not counting that I suppose I don't have a lot of reason to complain.

He brought me back a beautiful leather coat. He must a paid a fortune for it, by the price they are in the catalogue. He knows he couldn't afford that even with the money he was making. He said except for his board and what he sent home he saved practically every cent he had come in. That coat means a lot to me. Not that an item of clothes is going to make up for whatever it was we lost, but it do say a lot. Gord, I knows, was never someone who could come up with the right words.

The only thing is — you don't know how long it's going to last. If he can't come up with a job inside a month he'll be right back just like he was before. You mark my words. If he don't find a job, there's only one solution — we all moves to Alberta. And that's not something I could look forward to. At least here we got our own home.

I never had the nerve to tell him everything about Frank. I had to tell him just the same that it was in my mind about leaving. It come as a shock to him. I don't see why it should though, with what I had to put up with before he left. He wanted to know the reason. Was there another man is what his questions come down to. I never said yes and I never said no, because perhaps now there's not anymore. I don't know.

I'd like to give our marriage a chance at working again. I shouldn't give up on it that easy. If it was only Gord to think about it'd be different. I looks at Chris and I can see we're some of the reason he's got like he is. Rev. Wheaton was in the house Saturday night, and we sat in the kitchen, the three of us, and talked and talked. I'm almost ashamed to say it, but it took someone from outside the family for us to see why we got some of the problems we do with Chris. Whatever else you can say about Rev. Wheaton, and some'll tell you he's too quick with his tongue, he don't hide what's on his mind. We had no choice but own up to the fact that if Chris was getting out of control it was partly because he was seeing it better out around than what he had it at home. It's not all our fault just the same, because it's about time, he said, that Chris learned some responsibility too. Raising teenagers today is not easy. No, I said to him, and you can say that again.

FATHER

I'm like Lucy now, if there's one thing I'll say for Wheaton, he speaks hes mind. I'm glad he come over when he did because Lord only knows what else I might a said to Chris when I got around to it. When Lucy called me up in Alberta and said he was in trouble with the cops I was just about ready to kill it.

It don't surprise you half the time when you hears talk of someone else's youngster hauled up before court. You expects it the way some of them is reared up. But when you tries to raise your kids to be honest and they turns around then and gets into trouble like that, it makes you wonder.

I'll agree with Wheaton a hundred per cent. It's not something you can overlook and say it's not going to happen again — either going to court or what happened with that young fellow up to camp. That's how more trouble starts — they does something once and gets away with it and after that then it's go ahead and try something worse.

I knows it haven't been the best for him at

home. I realizes that. If I'd been able to live home I bet you he wouldn't a got into trouble like he did. Wheaton tried to say how it's been showed that alcohol is the reason for a lot of family problems. But if he was expecting a confession out of me he wasn't about to get one. He's going to have to do a lot of convincing to convince me I'm someone who drinks too much. There was times last winter and spring when I knows I was pretty steady at it. I'd be the first one to admit to that. But put any man through what I went through trying to come up with a job and just see if he don't look for something to take hes mind off hes troubles. I don't make no excuses. And perhaps the family did suffer for it. I'm not saying now they didn't. All I am saying is there was a reason behind it and Chris should a been smart enough to see it.

He's a pitiful sight today, all the same, when we leaves to go to court. You got to feel sorry for the young bugger in a way because he looks scared stiff the whole way in the car.

When we gets to Bakerton we got something like a half hour to spare. I figure I might as well go and have another talk with Manpower. They tells me now I won't know till Tuesday whether or not I've got the job I'm after. Yesterday it was Friday, now it's Tuesday. I told them I haven't got all friggin year to wait. I got to get something or go back to Alberta. I just can't afford to wait more than another week. This job I applied for only lasts six months. I figure if I can get it, then by that time perhaps they'll have their mind made up about the fish plant. I said to Lucy, it's either that or pack up and go. That is, if she's not packed up and gone off her own self by then. Although, from the way she's been talking I wouldn't say there's much chance of that now.

CHRIS

I guess I never ever figured I'd be turning up in a place like this. I can sure think of lot better ways to use up an afternoon. We've been sitting here an hour already and the case still haven't come up.

They got me charged with two things — drinking under age and wilful property damage. I guess I knows what I'm going to plead. I talked it out with the old man yesterday. I tried to make him see that it's still my word against theirs about the windows. He said how in the name of God could I expect an argument like that to stand up in court, considering how drunk I was at the time. I didn't come back with too great of an answer.

I bet they're doing this on purpose, making us wait. They probably think it's good for us to be suffering it out.

I takes a glance over at Stan and the other fellows. Stan's got a grin across his face. Seems like he's getting a great kick out of it. Then Dad looks across at him. He turns to me and by the expression on his face I can tell that if the old man had chance he'd probably ram a few knuckles down

Stan's throat.

I wish they'd get to us so we can get this over with. They've gone through three cases.

"Christopher Slade."

I mean, am I supposed to stand up or what? I didn't expect my name to be the first one called.

"Come forward and stand here."

One after another, all five names are read out. We're standing in front of the magistrate, behind a rail.

I'm not really as shitbaked as I looks.

The officer who did the investigation starts to read out a summary of the case. Sounds like the cop knows every detail. "Is there anything any of you would like to say at this time?" the magistrate asks when he finishes.

I pleads guilty. All the others do too.

I can see the fun part is yet to come. The magistrate looks each of us over. I guess you're sorta expected to look him straight in the face. I finds it awful hard to do that.

He starts off by talking about respecting other people's property. Then about how the law is not too keen on vandalism. My eyes wander to the floor.

"Do you understand what I'm saying?"

My head jumps back. "Me?"

"Yes, are you paying attention to what I'm say-ing?"

"Yes . . . sir."

"How old are you?"

"Sixteen."

"And is this your first time before court?"

"Yes, sir."

"And do you realize the seriousness of these charges?"

"Yes, sir."

"You know you're a very lucky young fellow. Of the five people standing here you're the only one who will walk out of this courtroom without a criminal record. That's because by law you're considered a minor. I hope you understand just how fortunate you are?"

"Yes, sir."

I don't try looking away from him a second time.

"Each of you will be put on a year's probation. The cost of repairing the damage will be divided equally among you, approximately $325 each." On top of that he slaps Stan with a $400 fine. I guess it didn't take much for him to figure out who was the ring-leader.

I wouldn't want to be in Stan's shoes. Three hundred and twenty-five bucks is bad enough. I wonder what Mom and the old man thinks of that.

Going back in the car, neither one of them says too much. I figure they know there's not much they could say that haven't been said already.

"I'll pay you back the money somehow," I tell them. "No matter how long it takes."

"Just keep yourself out of trouble, that's the main thing," the old man says.

"He'll be okay, don't worry about it," Mom says. It's Dad she's looking at when she's saying it. But it's me, I guess, who appreciates it the most.

21

JENNIFER

At least I won't look like the poorest one there when I show up at the university residence. A brand-new luggage set is not something I expected. Perhaps Dad was that overjoyed at the thoughts of seeing me go he didn't mind spending so much money. I shouldn't say that, I suppose. It is a cruel thing to be saying.

He's borrowed a car for an hour to drive me to where the bus stops on the highway. Chris gathers up enough interest to come along, although probably it's more for the ride than it is to see me off. He keeps talking to Dad about the size of the motor and how fast he thinks he could make her move if he was the one driving.

"Put her to the floor," he says, more to tease Mom than for any other reason. For Chris, that's the closest thing to anything friendly towards her that I've heard him say in two weeks. I haven't yet been able to pinpoint the reason for their being on such unfriendly terms. Of course Chris doesn't need much of a reason to be unfriendly with anybody. He's cooled off a lot from his little escapades this summer. I guess they finally managed to tame him down a few notches. Lately he's been keeping to himself a lot. He needs to, the trouble he got himself into. I'd be ashamed to show my face in public if I were him.

Mom is close to tears. She knows I've got to go. It's not as if I haven't been planning this for years. Last night she came into my room when I was packing and passed me a bank book in my name with over $500 in it. I told her she didn't have to go and do that, even though I knew all summer that's what she was up to. She says that much, plus the scholarship and the money I made this summer might get me through the first year without taking out any loan at all. More than likely it will. She knows I won't be wasting any money.

"As long as you works hard, that's the main thing. Don't be like some now — go in there for nothing only a good time. And if you needs anything, don't be afraid to ask for it. Or if you feels yourself getting lonely, just pick up the phone and call us collect."

She should know that there won't be much chance of that. Even though life around home hasn't been too bad this summer, at least not for me, I'm still looking forward to university and getting out on my own for a while. Marten is just too boring for me now.

When we get to the Irving station where the bus stops it's Dad's turn to quiz me about having everything I need. That's a switch. It's true, he's been different since he came home, but he knows

I don't forget that easily.

Still I have to say this much for him — he hasn't been drunk once since he got back, not even that first night when all the people were in the house. He wasn't any more than feeling good. I hope for Mom's sake he stays off it. We'll see by Christmas just how much will power he's got. He says to me, "Now, no matter where we are Christmas I'll send you the money for your passage." He's talking about if they go to Alberta. I think they should go myself. It'd do Mom good to get out and see a bit more of the world. She's never even been off the Island. I was out as far as Manitoba last year on a student exchange and I loved it.

It's not long before the bus shows up. It's only a five-minute stop so there's not much time for anything except getting the luggage to the driver and saying goodbye. Daryl is going into St. John's on the same bus and, of course, we've already made plans to sit together. He's going in to do electronics at the College of Trades and Tech. It's been over two months now since we started going out.

By the time I'm ready to board the bus, Mom's eyes are well reddened and I feel sad too to see how much my going away means to her. I squeeze her hard as she presses her lips to my cheek. Dad is standing there next to her. He looks awkward with his hand out. I kiss him on the cheek and say goodbye. It looks like he might want to kiss me back.

Chris, foolish as ever, is nothing but a grin.

"Goin to kiss me?" he says, knowing for sure I don't want to.

"I think I'll pass it up."

"Good, I won't have to wash my face twice today."

I think I've got stomach enough to pay him back for that. Before he has chance to move away I wrap my arm around his neck and make a very slobbery imprint on the side of his face.

It catches him by surprise. "Shit, you don't have to drown me."

"Just so we don't forget each other."

I kiss Mom once more and then I go up the steps. Our seats are on the other side of the bus, so as it leaves it's impossible for me to see either of them through the window.

CHRIS

Jennifer is gone. She went yesterday. I won't say it's good riddance, but one thing *is* okay — she's not in school this year.

I decided to go back and give school another try. I figured I might as well. The court bit is over, and now I knows where I stand, so this morning I showed up. Since school was open for four days last week, I figure I better go to Keats, the principal, the first thing and be the one to break the good news to him.

As you might guess, Keats don't exactly do a

somersault when he sees me come into his office. I apologize about the windows, even though I'm still not sure if I had any part in it. It happened that one of the ones smashed was in his office, and I can see where it's been replaced by a new one, the sticker and all still on it. I figure I might as well put in about going to court too, just in case he haven't heard. It might do something to cool down the speech that's sure to be coming.

Keats got no intention of disappointing me. I listens to it all. About how if I am coming back he's expecting better things from me. I don't say much to him, but the thing is — I've got my mind made up to put more effort into my school work this time around. That might be hard to believe, but it's true.

This determination don't even slack off when my streak of good luck continues and I ends up with Anderson again for math. I guess the 35 per cent I got on last year's final is still sorta cemented in his brain cells. The look he gives me when I turns up for his class the second period makes Keats look tame. Never mind Anderson, I'm thinking to myself, you'll get over that. I'm going to try to pass this time even though math still makes me sick.

There's a few people glad to see me back. None of them teachers though. Tompkins hunts me down during recess and lays on the big smile of his. "Knew you couldn't stay away," he says. "This place is just too great to pass up. This calls for a celebration Friday night."

"I'm cuttin down."

"Gone soft?" he says. I wonder who he learned that from?

"No, just goin to buy it by the half dozen," I laugh.

No, the truth is I really have it in my mind to lay off the beer and dope a bit, at least down from what I was before. I bet I could even give it up altogether if I wanted to bad enough. One thing is — I needs to try to save a few bucks. And I knows Susan don't get off on me having too much of either one of it, although I'm not about to tell Tompkins that.

Things are not about to turn perfect, but at least now I feels a bit better about the way everything is going than what I have for a long time. Susan is one of the main reasons for that. She's the best thing there is about going back to school. We're in the same class for four of the six subjects I'm doing and she's got this certain something, several things in fact, that tends to take my mind off the more boring parts of school.

Here she is crazy over this probation kid. That's a pretty stupid way of putting it and well, I'm not sure if she's exactly crazy over me, but I'm loving it whatever it is. We had a long talk about that last night on the phone. It don't matter to her that to some people I'm your juvenile delinquent type. She don't care she said, all she cares about is me going back to school. Her and the old man should team up. In the end I have to tell her yes, just to keep her quiet. She's some of the reason I went back, but like I said, I had my own mind made up to it first.

Susan is the first girl I ever went out with that I really got off on that much. And she's the first girl I ever decided to bring into the house while Mom and Dad are around. The last thing they're probably expecting is for me to show up with a girl. I've never told them anything about her. I have to practically drag her to get her to come in because she's nervous as hell about meeting them. I tell her to knock off being so foolish, it's only my parents.

I think they like her. It's a new experience for the both of them, seeing me sitting quietly with a girl while we're all watching TV. Mom figures she's got to get the details on just whose daughter she is and who else is in her family and what grade she's doing in school. Susan stands up pretty good to the torture test. The old man is happy enough to just crack a joke about how, when he was going out with Mom, her father wouldn't let him past the porch till he'd been going out with her for a year. You can't believe the old man, he's liable to say anything. For frig's sake, it's the first time he's met the girl and he tells her straight to her face how it looks like I got pretty fair taste. Susan starts to turn red when he says that, which is just what he wants.

She's got to be home by eight-thirty, but before we go I convince her to come down the hall and have a look at my bedroom. I don't have the guts yet to close the door behind her. It's not much to look at — an old Star Wars poster that needs to be thrown away and one of an over-dressed Cheryl Ladd. Susan sits on the corner of the bed and I rummages through the drawer till I comes up with the letter I promised I would show her. It's from Morrison. I told her already about everything that happened up at camp.

I was certainly glad he answered my letter. He told me how the doctor had let him out of the hospital three days after I left to come home. He's all right now he said, as good as ever. He better be telling the truth. He's back at the same foster home where he was before. He says he likes it there and that at Christmas he'll see his real mother. Sounds like he could be okay. I was thinking maybe if he wanted to, he could come out for a weekend sometime. I don't know what regulations they got about that. I think maybe I'll talk to the old lady when I gets around to it and see what she thinks of the idea.

I walks Susan home and we have about ten minutes out by the side of her house before she's got to go in. I makes the most of those ten minutes. She says she'll phone me up later.

Back at the house the TV is still blaring away. I sits down in the arm chair thinking about whether or not I should shut it off. If I do Mom is sure to wake up. They're both stretched out, sound asleep on the chesterfield. A tight squeeze — they have their heads at opposite ends. The old man's got his arm slung across her legs.

I figure I'll let them sleep. They always did like

a nap. Besides, the old man told me earlier on that he's getting up early so's he can be in Manpower when it opens. I hope by frig he gets a job. I don't want to see things getting loused up around here again.